Yates, Victor,
A love like blood /
[2015]
33305234599235
mh   10/18/16

a Love like Blood

VICTOR YATES

Hillmont Press
Los Angeles

WITHDRAWN

Copyright ©2015 by Victor Yates

All rights reserved. This book or any portion thereof may not be reproduced or used in any manner whatsoever without the express written permission of the publisher except for the use of brief quotations in a book review.

Printed in the United States of America
First Printing, 2015
ISBN-13: 978-0692553312
ISBN-10: 0692553312
Library of Congress Control Number: 2015955101

Hillmont Press
512 Evergreen Street Unit 305
Inglewood, CA 90302

a Love like Blood

I sing so they'll know I am not afraid.
Billy Holiday

I write so they'll know I am not afraid.
Victor Yates

Dedicated to Alkebulan and Desmond.
Wherever you are. I love you. Thank you.

And to E. Lynn Harris.
Wherever you are. I love you. Thank you.

And to my future sons.
Wherever you are. I love you. Thank you.

Contents

texture is smooth, unlike the rest of its pruned body. My left hand cradles the Nikon, gripping the lens, and I tuck my elbows into my sides. Hand placement is as significant as breath. His thumb squeaks against the plastic as he turns the page. My eye moves to the viewfinder, and the camera fades. Shlick shlick. A seductive sound to a faraway shot. I am preparing myself to ask him as he flips through my portfolio if I can photograph him in profile. His profile is six sharpened lines: nose, cheek, jaw, brow, and neck. His face, cream shirt, and tanned arms are a study in contrast. His picture would capture the essence of a perfectly formed man.

With aluminum in my hands, hard facts soften into mush. The red in the room unravels, Father's eyes follow, then the world outside of the frame. They float to the floor creating a mound of threads. Concentration sucks all the colors away. Only light, breath, sound, and Brett are left. Glass breaks him down into a seed. Here, in the red, he and I have one name, twins. We share the warmth of the womb with all of the gruesome knowledge of the world. Instead of unraveling with the room, the image in the lens slicks down my worn ends. The camera slips as I hear a crackling sound, and the neck strap saves it from breaking. My father could catch us questioning desire in the season of cicadas. His eyes see everything, except himself. Distant yelling proves he glued his feet to the back of the truck. Outside, a kid chuckles and I step back, but the baritone of Brett's voice bends me toward his face. The camera clicks again. My lens is a permission slip granting access into the intimate world between men. I kick a box on accident causing crushed newspapers to shake. The boxes closest to me read Reed's room, darkroom chemicals, kitchen,

Chapter 1

My first language was Somali, then English, then Spanish. Although I am not fluent in Spanish. Red was the first word that formed in my mouth. Mother would cross her hands at the wrists, making her thumbs kiss, and wiggled her fingers to mimic a pigeon. She cooed to catch my attention, but the color distracted me. Her ruby polish was candy to suck. Because I could taste it and feel bubbles the size of poppy seeds, I could assign it meaning. Now when I refer to the color red, I use the Spanish word instead. In English, the word on my tongue sounds similar to my father's name. The color is a constant in my life: red darkroom lights, grease pencils, rosary beads, blotches, tissues, and Father's eyes. For a moment we stare at each other, then Brett looks down in his lap at the coffin. Standing in the maroon room, I relish in removing my camera from its resting place. I hold the body the way Father taught me allowing aluminum to sink into my skin. My right hand curls into the handgrip. The and photo albums. Under photo albums, in parentheses, is Carsten's Room. I snuck out my portfolio from the last box. Photography is the one language I speak that helps me communicate with men who move at night.

"You're probably the only teenager that has one of these," he says, with his head down.

"You are probably right."

A smacking noise comes from his mouth, then he says, "I like this one. Who is she?"

"A girl I knew in Chicago."

The sounds our bodies make will dissolve into the house's bones and will remain here forever. Then, the smacking, swallowing of saliva, and cracking of bones will combine, creating new noises. A cut-up Polaroid of my ex-girlfriend has him stuck, staring into the past. Maybe he has a question about her laugh; however, I hope he is asking questions about the print on my pants. Blood, not floral, tribal, or tropical, is responsible for the shape. The scent of frankincense thickens in the air. Making myself as tiny as possible, I position him into portrait. But before I tap the shutter button, I look up, down, and beside him, checking if the corner exits can be improved. I search the viewfinder and move the camera so that the blue flag, draped over a box, is not in the frame. The panel behind him (and above the fireplace) splits the maroon with myrrh in shiny stripes and church lace in dull stripes. A design detail I would discover in a darling hotel. The house, far from that, is the oldest on Evergreen Street in Beverly Hills. The pipes of the suburb could be ripped up and planted in the other Beverly Hills, in California, with its air of plastic bourgeois exclusiveness. Soon the living room will be filled with unextravagant things like the donated couch, love seats, coffee table, lamps, milk jars, and headrests buried behind boxes on the truck.

The shadow of my arm cuts across the shadow of Brett's body making a cross. Through the camera lens, I study his shape. The line of his body breaks the lines in the background, projecting him forward. His athletic frame, his bullish face, the veneer of toughness, and the paint splatter on his uniform, slash what Father screams at me. *Funny* men are pretty vaginas with mustaches. Pretty and Brett are as far apart as never and always. Mannified is a more accurate description. He is the type, which, when I see, I assume reeks of beer, cigarettes, and cheap after-shave. Though mannified men are always significantly older. Brett shines, not from the sun, from a readiness to show off his youth. When his father told my father he was eighteen, I asked him to stand on the other side of a bulky box. In response, he said *cool*. Cool is not in my vocabulary. Father prohibits me from using the language of my generation.

The ends of his curly hair are blond and hide the clues of his glances. Looking and liking have striking differences. He crosses his arms, one hand on his arm, and one hand tucked under his arm. "We're alike in different ways."

"How so?"

"We both work with our hands. I work with my dad in construction. You work with yours in photography. If you want to go to the Detroit art museum, I'll go with you."

"The DIA? I would live in a broom closet there. All those gorgeous silver prints."

"Let's do it," he says, lower and slower, sexual-sounding. "I can't believe you're a family of photographers."

"Two of us are photographers. My older brother isn't interested in photography. My younger brother wants to be a kid. I did not have a choice."

"I can tell your older brother and dad don't get along. You seem to somewhat."

"I do not have a choice with that either."

"Yes, you do."

"My father is Somali. You'll learn quickly. The photograph is the only thing I can control. I control what is going on inside it."

"The photo of the wedding dress and tux suspended in the air. And the two grooms holding a cross is beautiful. How'd you do that?"

"With lighting clamps. I clamped the dress and tuxedo onto a metal rod. And I asked two men in the wedding party we were shooting to pose together."

"Were they a couple?"

"No, but they had similar faces. I wanted to play with those images."

"Your dad must be proud of your work."

"He hasn't seen that picture."

"Why not?"

"He'd rip it in half. Anything he disapproves of, he destroys."

"How does it feel, to be reminded, of what you can't do?"

"What do you mean?"

"Have your dad photograph your wedding."

"Can I photograph you?" I ask him, to avoid answering his question.

"Yes." The word, a short intake of breath, pushed out in exaggeration to sound suggestive.

I break eye contact with him, pulling myself back. His explain something explicit is growing inside of him — something un-African, a sexual thought, material for an erection. I have studied that knowing-slant in the pages of a magazine that is a penis away from being pornographic. *Muscle Workout* might cause untrained eyes to miss it rummaging through my underwear drawer. This month's first workout, featuring a gymnast in fishnet swimwear, caused a woman to huff passing behind me in the grocery store. Turned, standing in profile, with the shutter speed narrow, Brett will appear bright and well-exposed. The background will come out dark, almost black, yanking out a wild ferocity in him, which will contrast with his feminine mannerisms. How his skin will look on film, I am not as certain. Being that Brett is biracial, his color drifts from tan to brown, depending on how much light hits his face.

In the lower corner of the frame, I catch the Somali flag with the five-pointed Star of Unity. Under it, there is a green flag with a crescent moon and star. I grew up in a strange world with Saint statuettes from my mother's mother alongside a Quran, wrapped in green silk that my father's father read from as a boy. In the upper frame, a moth appears and disappears fluttering over the oatmeal carpet. Every straight line is broken from this angle.

As the camera clicks, Brett uncrosses his arms and crosses them highlighting his neck, chest, and shoulders. If Father were hovering beside me, he would yell, stop, girls do that. His words are too pointed to forget, like the front-page of a newspaper during wartime. The light dazzles Brett's eyes and five brilliant flecks shine. *Wait*, I hold up a finger, pausing him, to shoot another picture and drag out this moment that we have alone. The first shot that a photographer takes is always a throwaway, like the peel of an unripe pomegranate, beautiful but unusable. I learned my greatest secrets from my Father and also ways to keep them. A musty scent enters the room with cut grass and an old dwelling smell. Close by, I hear tape ripping from a box. The splitting sound sends Father's fist flying toward my face, even though he is not physically in front of me. I listen for the tap tap of his shoes by the front door. Smooth as a cat on a carpet, he could tiptoe in on us to check where our hands are. If jolted he might bite them off. Death in his mouth is like cinnamon tea. The ride here held us under mirrors and heat and rattled him beyond his cattish ways. Indoor cats that escape outside will hunt and kill rats.

Rubbing his hands together, he grins as if he is about to say something off-color. "Do I need to marry you to see these pictures?"

Brett and I both laugh at this understanding between us, but this is a secret we have to toss into the fire.

Drizzled drops of paint highlight the veins in his right hand. By his middle knuckle, dried blood has crusted around a bruise. If the color red had a smell, it would smell metallic. A close-up shot of his hand, clearly focused, that is the photograph I need. His hand is the object that reveals we are native sons. And, we work out of the disorder of life to achieve beauty. I want to explore more.

Although, like the Nile crocodile, heavily armored and quiet until it attacks, Father creeps up on us.

"You, your father wants you," he says to Brett.

The coldness in his first word is enough for me to see my error. A photographer never stops looking. His eyes, usually expressionless, move toward perplexity. As the front door crunches, I realize the closest exit is a cracked

Chapter 2

Inside congested markets selling curry-flavored worms, images of disembodied hands are everywhere – in logos, pottery, graffiti, tattoos, jewelry, clothing, and charms. The image symbolizes protection. In Lama Doonka, where my grandfather is from, the symbol is eight-fingered. Finding villagers with six or seven fingers is as common as finding a traveling troupe of baboons. Eight-fingered villagers are treated like gods but are born once every one hundred years. My Father's unshakeable nickname growing up on the far North Side of Chicago was "Hand." His crueler friends would make tongue-clicking sounds around his name as if dressing it in quotes, but he smiled hearing it. Some of his closest childhood friends have only recently discovered why the nickname stuck. And, he smiles telling them. He moved like a professional illusionist, distracting them with overexaggerated gestures, pulling attention to his left side. The performance prevented them from gasping for breath at his right hand.

The human eye is easy to mislead, but cameras tell the truth or a distorted version of the truth. Of the thousands of photographs that I have of him, in only two are his right hand entirely visible. The first is a wedding picture buried in a bottom bedroom drawer. His hand is blurry and unremarkable from the wide angle of the living room. In the second picture, he is looming in Union Station inside the marble terminal. Tight concentration is in his face, and a Nikon camera is in his hand. He is photographing an older man in secret that is photographing his adult son. The son, partly in shadow, is cradling an infant in the crook of his arm at a slight incline. A dark-colored blanket insinuates the child's sex. Shot from his right side, the focal point of the image is my father. A crack in the tile runs from the top of his hand and connects him to the other men like a vein; it is closer to the skin. From son to father and father to son, our relationships are equal in blood; however, our trinities are unrelated and unknowable. Five or six once-overs might be required to realize that his hand looks rather peculiar, and then the viewer notices it: skin, soft tissue, a bone with a joint, two thumbs. Fortunately, the crash of noise and Father's concentration muted the clicks of my camera.

Water plopped in fours somewhere inside my high school's darkroom. The room felt restrictive from its arrangement of tables. It smelled older too than the rest of the school as if it had been torn out of another building and dropped into ours. Or maybe the room had been born a restroom, and the adjacent storage room walls were hammered into dust. Dust, dirt, moisture, and hands age restrooms faster than other rooms. In the other prints from Union Station, I rubbed my fingers across Father's eyes, feeling for familiarity. But I only found the disconnected stare of a man to self-involved to care about anyone else but his lover, his work. Though someone else who saw the pictures might think, that he had found a new way of talking in silence. My fingers wrinkled like an elderly man's by the time the pictures had dried. I tried to mimic the intensity on his face without a mirror to face. The way lines creased in the space between his eyebrows and the beginning of his nose; I could not copy, even when mashing the points together. A microwave beeped three times on the other side of the wall where I stood. Something like a saucer or coffee mug scraped the glass, and a minute later, I handed my life to my instructor.

"Hands are more expressive than faces. You've captured that here," he said.

Weeks later, he added the photograph was one of my strongest during a portfolio review. Then, he pulled it closer and rubbed his lips with his finger. While watching his lips mouth soundless words, I missed him reaching into his desk and realized this after a magnifying glass smashed my father's head. What the magnifying glass could not show, being in black and white, was the blood under his thumb, nor the spotted tissue beside my foot. The photograph embodies every lesson that I have learned from Father as a photographer – from image structure and contrast and balance to darkroom editing and hand placement. A real education is unconscious seduction. Want and risk in wanting wait under the laurel wreath. However, Father has never seen the print and never will, hopefully. He would rip it up into a million little pieces and demand I hand over the negative.

Chapter 3

Through the fisheye peephole, the crimson and clay-colored world kindles under the late afternoon sun. Careful not to cause a sound, I crack the door and peek out, listening for the tap tap of church shoes. A watch ticks. My knee bangs against the doorframe. Purple leaves on a head-high shrub shake. I jerk back, seeing a hand move, and relax. Brett nods, standing at the bottom of the steps.

"I'll help you," he says.

Tiptoeing down into danger, I glance in both directions first. Then, I leap looking towards Brett's house; however, he loops his arm around my arm. Now, I cannot disappear. The puffed-up paint splatter itches rubbing against my skin. Glancing at the truck and then his face, I stop convinced I am with an aged version of him. Somehow time has sped up and spun a net around him, plucking out his youth as if it were nose hairs. His face was mannified, although now it is gaunt. The skin under his eyes looks hollow. In his eyes, fear appears to be a foreign feeling. His boots march on the path toward an enemy, whose hands are sharper than thorns. A flattened box spins in the air from the back of the truck to the driveway. Red-bricked and with cobweb cracks, the driveway is a reminder of Father's violence. The bloated inside of the truck is a visual catalog of his madness. On the seven-hour drive, every pothole that rattled the wheels was a fist in my gut. I convinced myself that the sardined furniture was crushing up my cameras. Being pig-headed, he selected the mid-sized rental over the longer truck that we needed to save eight dollars and forty-five cents. Two bloody tissues slide on top of a box labeled hot lights from boxes moving. Scuff marks cover the outside. Lenses and, under the word, for the studio, is written in parenthesis on the box to my right. Father's forehead wrinkles pushing a bundle of light stands to the truck's edge. A burlap rice sack is wrapped around the stands, and the bundle is tied together with an electrical cord. Each stand weighs thirty pounds to support heavier photography equipment. The sack, cord, and stands can turn into instruments of torture at any moment. Brett and I grab opposite ends of the sack together in a synchronized movement.

"Stop. He doesn't need your help," Father says.

"Mr. Tynes, yes he does."

"No, he doesn't. He needs to stop being weak."

Glassy-eyed and focusing his fury on me, he tucks his left fist under his right triceps and his right fist under his left triceps. His way is the only way a man should cross his arms, according to him. The gesture is a period at the end of a sentence that does not need words. An entire non-verbal vocabulary exists for his violence.

"No, I can manage," I say to Brett.

Hesitating at first, he sets his side of the sack down at a long-drawn-out pace. Father's eyes throw daggers at the damned world beneath his worn sandals. The thick layer of shea butter that I smoothed over my face is sweating off in the Midwest heat. Milky beads drip to the sack. My thin shirt sticks to my chest and back while I fight with myself how to hold the stands. I struggle to carry them, cradled in my arms, for five feet and stop.

From across the yard, Brett's blond father says, "help him," with a buttery tenderness that is unfamiliar to my ears.

He waddles to the truck with two paint buckets in one hand and a toolbox in the other. Brett smirks as Father nods down at us and spits. I close my eyes before the pink goo splats on the ground. Father's face is stone but pockmarked with resentment. The irony is that now he will bless Brett helping me out of respect for his father. Somali men refuse to shame other men to their face. The resentment in his face settles into blankness. Even without a mirror to verify it, I know my face is as blank as his. Brett's face reverses back into his youth.

Our bodies, ready for the job at hand, float up from the cobwebs. The purple leaves shake as they scrape my arm. Glancing over my shoulder, I step inside the warm living room and look in front of me and fixate on Brett's body. Muscle fibers in his arms fill up with blood, showing off his veins. His veins twist like politics on his skin. Blood rushes between my legs as we lower the stands to the floor. The lines of his jeans are swollen with puberty and milk. I ask in secret with my hands to show me what is underneath. Turning my back to Brett, I adjust myself through my khakis and move it up into a less noticeable position. His face is a face that I know and do not know.

Athletic, hirsute, strong-featured, and with large feet, he is every combination of the men featured in my non-porn porn collection. The videotapes, which are exercise workouts, are in the last place my father would rummage through, a satchel with an angel's face printed on the front and back.

With my back to Brett, I say, "It will probably take us all day to unload everything."

"Can I ask you something? How do you deal with your dad's cruelness?"

I start to respond, but the truth might frighten him. My second answer feels dishonest and borrowed. That is the difficulty with language, finding the purest way to describe emotions, without having the appearance of stealing rented words. But then again, he should be as terrified as I am. My father is capable of anything, even killing a child. Brett only knows his father, paint, hammers, wood, and the splinters in his hands.

In my silence, Brett says, "You need to stand up to him."

I shake my head in agreement; however, I know the moment I fight my Father, will be the moment he pulverizes my body into a soupy pulp. Yes, I have wanted to say – curse word – you to him two hundred times today, but my brothers and I are not allowed to swear. Respectable Catholics cannot pollute God's breath with disrespectful language, especially Black Cuban Catholics.

"You need to speak up for yourself."

"It is not that simple. Your father is not Somali. If he were, you would understand."

"You shouldn't put up with his bullshit."

A soft rattling like ice shaking in a plastic cup startles me. The pain in my face forces my feet to take a small step to the right away from Brett. I take another step. Junior, my older brother and Father's favorite son, tugs the dolly into the living room. Brett whispers something, but the words sound like gibberish. White bungee cords secure four boxes down to the dolly by its handle. My younger brother speed walks around Junior huffing, carrying two black-framed posters.

"Here," Ricky says, leaning the blown-up photographs forward for me to grab, and then he races up the stairs, pumping his arms up in the air.

"Who is this?" Brett asks, pointing to the woman posed in the first poster.

"Marian Anderson. Richard Avedon, my idol, shot this."

The black and white image has a gypsy-like quality. Strings of multi-shaded beads are around Marian's neck. Her long, jet-black hair streams across her high cheekbones. Her hair is wild and windswept and elegant. The first time I stumbled upon this picture at Whitney Museum, I had to reread the description five times. In every other picture of the opera singer I had seen, she had perfectly coiffed hair, was put together, sequined, furred, ready to sing a standing ovation worthy performance. This picture, shot from the neck up, is unflattering, makeup-less, focused on her voice. She is singing to Richard against a stark white background. Later that day, I bought every album of hers that I could find at a music store down the street from the museum.

Junior heaves, straining himself, setting one of the boxes on the ground. A noise follows that only a man designed like him can release in public – he breaks wind. Being pudgy and drab, he could tumble into a pool of pink glitter and sashay out wearing a tiara and tutu, and no one would question his manhood. That may be the reason Father wants to mold me into a younger version of Junior; being that Junior is a younger version of Father.

"If you're free tomorrow," I say to Brett. "We will be setting up our studio in downtown on Main."

I regret saying it as it leaves my lips.

Brett rubs the back of his curly head in a slow, forward sweep to his forehead, down to his face and spreads his fingers open. The gesture is seductive and playful. He pinches his nose, cocks his head up saying, "downtown," and shakes his head no.

And, I am grateful for that answer.

As we walk back outside, the scent of rosemary weighs down the warm air. Brett drapes his arm around my shoulder in a graceful movement. A quiet celebration is happening, but I want to continue away from the eyes of everyone else. This physical closeness, might appear vulgar to my father, and lead to punches. Natural excitement turns to terror as his arm remains in place. If I move out of his embrace, that might confuse him. Step, step, and I can almost catch a glimpse of the back of the truck, where my father is praying. I slow my pace, but my legs tremble. Father's soaked back is facing us. The pressure of his hand lightens sliding down my body. I snatch my hand away as he squeezes it. Father spins around holding a box that he insisted I tape up earlier. A resealable bag, matchsticks, frankincense, two chunks of charcoal, an incense burner with one handle, and a bundle of dried sage (to bless the house) are inside it. Inside the resealable bag, there are spearmint leaves, black tea leaves, khat leaves, cardamom powder, and a smaller bag with pills.

"Young man, your father, said you needed to be somewhere right now," Father says.

"I completely forgot," Brett says and checks his sports watch. Pink flashes itself, a pig pink, like where babies come from, and a finger increases its size. The rubber band on his wrist is a rainbow: pink leads to purple, purple leads to soft blue and soft blue leads to pink.

"He already left. You should go," Father says. "And thank your father for the cart. I'll grab it. Junior," Father yells as loud as he can toward the house. "Bring that cart back."

"Keep it. You still have more to move," Brett says. "Nice meeting you Mr. Tynes and Carsten."

At the touch of his calloused hand, I transform into a boy disconnected from his prepubescent body. Blood engorges between my legs, and I become firmer and enlarged and it is impossible to disguise it with Brett shaking my hand. As his hand lowers, his eyes also lower. I dig my sweaty hands in my pocket to readjust myself. My body, having a built-in alarm clock between my legs, buzzes and vibrates when it finds a man attractive. I am not certain; however if I will be able to reveal to my Father that I am attracted to men.

With his right hand, Father taps his forehead, then his chest, his left shoulder, then his right shoulder and the boxes behind him become an altar.

"Carsten," he says in a tone reserved for lessons on manhood. "Carsten," he screams and kicks me in the shoulder. "Don't hang out with that boy. He's khaniis."

Hearing that abrasive word forces me to remember every lie that I have torn from my tongue, and given to my Father in the past year.

Chapter 4

The ribs of a photography umbrella are comparable to a human rib cage, in that one break disturbs the way a photograph breathes. The sensation of breaking ribs, little snaps, like cowpea beans being torn open, is as familiar to me as the smoothness of my camera's shutter button. Two summers ago in 1996, I shot four rolls of film at the beach, where Lake Shore ends, at a curve and turns into Sheridan Road. I caught a city bus and stopped at Ardmore. From Ardmore, I caught a glimpse of blonde sand, blue water, and handsome men in Speedos. Six miles away, Father was shooting the wedding of two Somali families from our neighborhood. He asked me not to shoot with him and said that he would return to the studio later that night.

When I heard the three bells ding on the front door, I started snatching the photographs out of the drying rack. Father barged into the darkroom and glanced at the last picture as I was reaching for it. In the picture, two blond bodybuilders in Speedos were in a classic beefcake pose. Both bodybuilders had one arm flexed, and the other extended up and out to the side. Father had my body pinned down on the studio's hardwood floor before I could run out to Michigan Avenue, and disappear in the breath of the city. My chest cracked, easy as eggs, from the punches. The feeling afterwards: a gravedigger's shovel splatting against dirt. I tasted metal in my mouth. Father broke me down as if I would be born again and made perfect. The colors in the room were sucked out and turned bone. I heard tapping, followed by distant voices. I woke up stiff on a cushionless examine table, with Father whispering, "don't tell her," in my ear. I obeyed his order and did not reveal to the nurse that he broke my ribs.

The next day, he handed me an expensive camera, now my favorite hush hush camera and told me, "I love you. I'm sorry," in Somali. The sentences sounded more like you are a prisoner, in being that I felt like a prisoner. To break away from under the bounds of his power, I snapped every rib on his most-beloved photography umbrella. Sharp pains shot from my chest to my shoulder as I broke his ribs; however, I could not stop. It was the first time I felt confidence radiating in my body without a camera in my hand. What was strange was that when he discovered what I did, he cleaned up the shredded nylon without saying a word.

Chapter 5

Metal toys hit the ground in an explosion of rage, underlining Father's last word – a sexual slur in Somali. My older brother's face begs me to bark back at him. My younger brother smoothes out the bottom of the split open box. The tape crinkles. His fingernails click against vintage dump trucks, race cars, and trains as he snatches them up. On each beat, Father's eyes blink, and then they squint at me becoming thin slits. The slits widen and become ravens. He wipes his nose with his wrist and wraps his other hand over the redness. Lean-jawed, his face slick with shea butter, a plant leaf stuck between his teeth, he only knows hunger and disappointment.

Looking at his watch, he screams, "what is taking so long?" a second time.

"Say something," Junior whispers to me, showing off his missing tooth.

"Do you have something to say?" he asks, with his heat singeing Junior then me.

In the silence, Junior mumbles Father's least favorite curse word. On cue, Ricky reverses out of the adult world, leaving the sound of metal jangling from inside the box. Green juice dribbles down the edge of Father's mouth. He coughs, spits a stream of green, and jumps in Junior's face as the jangling dies. The familiar mint and citrus scent of khat leaves makes my tongue itch.

"I could kill you right now." Father screams.

"Moving everything off that fast is impossible," I blurt out.

"Only a woman would say that. Move it in five minutes. Or you will be sleeping in the truck tonight."

The word you, in Father's mouth, stings worse than a wasp. I limp in pain toward the door, propped open by a bronze rooster. The pearl bone glints around his neck. The pearl is a talisman that can steal a sick child back from death if the child rubs it, according to superstition. For the past half hour, Junior and I have broken our backs moving the couch, clock, cabinets, stereo system, and larger boxes without stopping. Brokenness is not enough for him. Pushing past the veil of frailty is his idea of performance.

"Don't suck your teeth like a girl," Father yells.

"Why do you talk to him like that?" Junior yells back.

"Because he's my son. Carsten. Stop," he yells.

I ignore him limping outside bloated with the burden of Blackness. My absence will leave him empty handed with nothing physical to crush. All I know from Father is screaming, pain, finger stains, and religion. Knowing these things, I ignore the knots in my legs and run.

With the passion of a street preacher, fanatic for the word, he yells, "you woman."

"You're the woman. You haven't moved one thing," Junior yells.

Whomp, I hear, like a fist tearing into flesh, then the floor groans under Father's weight as he chases after me. In the hurry not to fight, I kick over a box on the steps, yanking myself up with an invisible string. Months old issues of *Chicago Woman* spill out onto the bricks and split apart at the spine. A magazine Father has freelanced for, on and off, since 1985. When his camera is not cradled in his hands, he likes to spit out woman, little girl, feminine, at me, the way village elders shoot out canuuni fruit seeds from their mouths. Both are equally ugly to witness. I stare at my reflection in the window of the car that we hitched here. The same car where I learned to pop my dislocated shoulder back into place. Seeing my father, grieving over women with shoe prints on their smiles, I want to smash the glass. I glance over my shoulder and Junior brushes past him, revealing red spots near the top of his white shirt. I realize that the spots are blood. For my brother, blood means punch back and harder. My reaction is the complete opposite – to run. A box clatters crashing closer to the house, and I push through the pain. Our old life will live in our new house through the arrangement of furniture, and that thought ungrounds me.

Inside the garage next door, Brett drops a battered bag into the bed of a pickup truck. A dust cloud trembles as it climbs up into the summer air. He grunts grabbing another bag. From the sidewalk, I darken the lines in the background and blur the shapes around them. Habit moves me to pat my chest, although my camera is not strapped around my neck. Watching him from this distance reduces the redness of the color red. Six silver-framed certificates show Contractor of the Year, Fuller Construction Company, beginning in 1989 and ending last year in 1997. A built-in cabinet with eighteen doors extends the entire length of the back wall. An enlarged picture of Brett, his father, and another blond floats in the center of the doorless middle section. The other blond resembles Brett's father. Brett's graphic t-shirt has the headless torso of a male bodybuilder with a swollen chest. His smile is the smile of my childhood. The men are comfortable, holding him in one arm hugs. Their smiles are smiles to remember. However long that he has this image, he has proof that his father loved him as he was.

"Tired of moving boxes?" he asks me.

"No, I am tired of my father calling me a girl."

"Stand up to him."

"And then what?"

"You'll find out what happens."

"I know what will happen."

"How?"

"I am his son."

"Okay," he says, interrupting me. "Can you help me?" He points to about twenty bags of cement mix on the black marked floor.

With the tan bags, neatly arranged on the truck, they resemble the flour sacks that are abundant in African villages. The blue USAID stamp stands out against the burlap and the brown-dominated landscape. Villagers feed their family's flatbread and fried sweet bread with the flour. Now, I can taste the cardamom, honey, spiced butter, powdered sugar, papaya jam, and khat tea in my mouth. In October, during our last visit, a group of men set two males discovered having sex on fire with two hundred flour sacks. A blistered message that same-sex desire is a Western disease, imported and caught as if a cold, and cured through a blaze. Their faces were inhuman: fathers, grandfathers, and dirty-faced boys as young as seven. They all knew these two men and had loved them, and no one in the crowd cried. Hate is thick in our blood. Around my seventh birthday, Father found out that his younger brother kissed another boy and beat him to the point that he became blind in one eye. Junior regurgitated the grisly details of the fight and punctuated the conversation with, "if he could attack his brother, then he could kill a son." His words imprisoned me in an idea-walled cell. Often, long-term prisoners commit suicide when their requests for parole return denied. Recently, I started asking myself, what if I remain in confinement forever from Father forcing me to marry my ex-girlfriend. In those moments, death seems to be the quickest way to unglue the cinderblocks.

Paint fumes blend with the ammonia smell from the cement mix and release a noxious odor. The scent is similar to the smells of the darkroom. Dust from holes in the bags stick to my arms and onto Brett's shirt. His shirt has a starch-like stiffness, probably from being worn multiple times without being washed. I love his roughness. Staring at the dark silky hairs around his lips, I realize what attracts me to him. It is his movement between masculine and feminine. At first his sexuality was a question mark blinking in front of me, because of his manly appearance and effeminate behaviors. There is a disquieting beauty to the contrast, even more so with the construction hat on his head and the dangling curls in his face.

"This is a beautiful truck."

"I'll take you for a ride whenever you want."

"Does your father let you borrow it?"

"It's mine. I bought it with cash I saved working for him."

"I put all my money into cameras."

"That's what makes us different. I rebel out in the open. You are sweating. Let me get you some water."

He caresses my forehead. I flinch, not from the roughness of his hand, but from being unprepared. My skin prickles from the softness of his gift. Like the sun on my face, like sweet Sycamore figs and guava paste, I love how I feel under his influence. I want to hear his breath in my ear as I stare at the dotted globs of paint on the ceiling. Clasped, but without metal joining them, our hands would connect us, the way sexual organs cannot. He disappears into the house through the side door. Working photographers know the power of place. The way a photographer stands in front of his subject affects the photograph. And the way a photographer holds a camera also has an effect. If cameras dream, they dream to be touched by someone like him.

The sensual shape of a wrench casts a shadow over Brett's face in the photograph. With my eyes closed, I try to focus in on the aspects that excite me – the pink bandanna around his head. The way his nipples poke out of the bodybuilder's chest and the ampleness of his hips accentuated by his crossed legs. The eyes, filled with black sex and white powder, have been dazzled by the sun. He is taller than my father, approximately my height, and also could be considered older. Like a cactus that blooms late at night, he stands erect, ready, showing off a pink opening at the end of a tube. The act is beautiful while it lasts; however, the witness is unlikely to experience it again. A pocketknife, with the blade out, is under the picture on the shelf. A spreading coldness on my back shocks me. I snap around. He nods, head up, holding out a water bottle. As our hands touch in the giving, a splotch at the bottom of my palm distracts me, and I drop the bottle. Nowhere else do I see maroon.

"There's a photo exhibit at the museum," he says and picks up the bottle. "I drove by a billboard for it yesterday. We can go on Saturday."

"I will let you know."

"Okay. Can you bring your camera?"

The word can so close to camera conjures khaniis up from the dead, and its thorns disrupt the conversation. I watch the word hovering above Brett. I want to choke it and leave it unfruitful. However, then, I hear the word flaming in my ear and the second word materializes on top of the first. More words appear. Maricon. Broke-wristed. Sweet booty. Soft. Sugar in the tank. Fruity. Funny people. Skeef. I imagine a fat-lipped vagina smacking open in between my legs, every time Father screams skeef. The coarseness of that word transforms how I see myself. I have to prove that I am separate from it, not because I am not attracted to men, but because Somali boys are divined to become fathers. And, fathers' bodies are like God's body. The body of an ungodly man is a coffin. Every time a woman we know womb expands for a baby, her family prays for a boy. Boys are kings that can increase their family's wealth. One boy is worth five girls. One skeef is worse than having five unmarriable daughters. To say the word, emphasis is placed on the first four letters – skee (it should sound like a hiss) and followed by if. Then, add the ferocity of hungered people, and even ears that have never touched the Horn of Africa with their bare feet can hear women pounding sorghum with wooden mortars and pestles. They can hear it because the clamorous children have been startled into silence.

Seeing these slurs glued together as if they are a bridge to eternal damnation, I tell Brett, "I should leave" and the soft air of sadness dissolves the letters into a handful of dust.

Chapter 6

Stolen gooey creams, gritty scrubs, and slimy masks were my G.I. Joes years ago. I was a child soldier stealing for beauty. When no one was looking, I would dab cream under my eyes, at the bone, as if war paint and smear umber and verdigris clay on my body as if camouflage. I needed their language, their textures, and possibilities. Maroon blotches covered my face, arms, and legs yet my Mother, Father, and brother had even skin. The blotches had the appearance of inflamed freckles but were larger than freckles and smaller than a child's front tooth. Our family doctor told Father stress was causing the blotches. Father laughed in his face while Junior invented a new nickname for me, Chester Cheetah. He would sneak and hide behind corners in our apartment, jump out, and scream, "It ain't easy being cheesy." I was seven then. Now I cannot walk down the snack aisle in grocery stores. Orange bags of cheese puffs cause my skin to itch, and I hear Father's laugh and see the way he looked at the doctor, like a deranged man.

Four weeks after my eighth birthday, father dropped Junior and I off at an Ethiopian-owned barbershop. I was sitting in the barber's chair, caped, staring at the hair-covered floor. The barber angled my head down to line up the thick hair on my neck. A confident man paraded into the crowded barbershop wearing faded jean shorts. I marveled at his body from the knees down. His legs were enviable, smooth and bright brown, like a brand new penny with golden undertones. Nothing else could hold my attention. The barber swung the vinyl chair around, and I faced the mirror at his black lacquered station. I stared at the man's magazine-ready legs. His legs glowed even more in the mirror.

Later that night, when Father was talking on the phone in the living room, I snuck into my parent's bathroom. I found a fading cream that I had not seen in the back of the cabinet under the sink. The front of the bottle had an elegant seahorse insignia and the word unblemished prominently printed. The word shimmered with flecks of silver. I smuggled the bottle into the guest bathroom and savored slathering the buttery cream on my legs. Then, I smothered my face with cream. The cream had the consistency of mashed avocado, and it smelled clean. My cheetah rosettes looked less maroon and more medium brown, about twenty minutes later. I applied more to my face. The blotches turned a shade lighter. I applied even more. Rubbing the cream into my skin, I felt a wave of heat, followed by tranquilness, and finally a sensation of an unending euphoria. Even though all the treatments were different, their labels had a shared language: unblemished, clear, healthy, glowing, gorgeous, and beautiful. The word beautiful was always in the description. I knew how valuable the word beauty was. Beauty equaled immunity from Father's rage. His cameras were beautiful to him, and he loved them more than anything else in his life.

As I turned on the sink faucet, Father barged into the guest bathroom.

"If I catch you playing in these again, I'll cut off your hands," Father yelled and smacked my head. I fell to the white tiled floor. Blood dripped from a cut on my face. Father dragged my body to the toilet and shoved my hands into the bowl. He yanked out my hands, and as I struggled, he forced me to wipe the white cream off my face with water from the toilet.

"You should be in the darkroom," Father yelled and left.

As I inhaled stale urine from the toilet, I realized that to receive Father's love photography would have to become my passion. I knew I would have to become comfortable watching the world develop in trays, even when waves rocked the surface.

Chapter 7

Dried clay flakes, fragile as a spider's web, fall to the blue bed sheet. The flakes resemble cooled ashes. With each flake, the treatment removes a flaw. Gray guck is caked in-between my fingers and in the lines on my right hand. Gently, with my middle finger, I circle the spot by my Adam's apple where a blotch appeared earlier. From the way I am lying, at the foot of the bed, I catch my reflection in the bathroom mirror. A slender plastic tube, a straight-sided glass jar, and a round jar christen the bathroom counter and will vanish before Father returns. Creams combined with aloe vera jelly, sticky vitamin E, and slimy banana peels can minimize cuts, scrapes, and black eyes.

The detailed directions on the round jar suggest I should have washed my sunburned face twenty minutes ago. Ten minutes longer and I will wash the mask off. Ten minutes of shooting can produce more provocative work than five hours of shooting. I learned that from Father, and he learned it from Grandfather, who beat it into him. Grandfather first handed Father a camera when he was five. At five, I received my first camera, a Land Polaroid. When Father turned eighteen, he married Mother at a neighbor's house. Grandfather used the same Land Polaroid to shoot my parent's wedding along with fancier equipment. My older family members, on Father's side, have traditionally married at eighteen. Grandfather married Grandmother at eighteen. Grandfather's seven siblings were married at eighteen also. There are only two exceptions – Junior and our uncle. I am a year away from marriage age, and every wrinkled face in my life is bullying me into a rented tuxedo to marry my ex-girlfriend. However, the feel of coarse facial hair rubbing against my jaw arouses me; not breasts, blunt bangs, lace, or lipstick. I shape my mouth into an O like Marian Anderson. I laid Marian propped against the unpainted wall with twenty other framed photographs. In the stack, only one photograph is not my own. My hand bumps against a solid object at the foot of the bed – my favorite camera. The black enamel paint has rubbed off in certain areas due to extensive use. The way the camera grips in my hand builds an intimate shooting experience. I trust this Nikon more than I trust my father. Yesterday, I shot Brett with this same camera. Tomorrow night I will convert my bathroom into a makeshift darkroom and develop the suggestive roll of film. I cannot let Father find these pictures. No lie would hide the intimacy in them. Once the film is developed, I will sneak over to Brett's with my camera when Father has fallen asleep. Like wallet, bus fare, keys, an essential, a camera's in my hand or around my neck when I leave home.

A paint roller, box cutter, five paint cans, white bed sheets, and a cardboard box labeled Carsten's room are in the corner opposite from the door. Earlier today, I sliced open the box and hid all the beauty products inside the box under the bathroom sink behind a wall of cleaning supplies. Then, I snuck out of the house. Brett persuaded me to run with him to downtown Beverly Hills. It turned into a tour of his favorite hardware store, his favorite music store, his favorite ice cream shop, and his favorite deli, Havington, which is across the street from the photography studio. As we passed the studio, I pinched Brett's puffy nipple poking out through his work shirt. He chased me into a verdant park that had a canine sculpture made of mirrored tiles. In the mirrors, I noticed the maroon blotch on my neck. I told Brett I needed to hurry back home, and I ran and did not stop until I reached my bathroom. By then, most of my neck was red. When I laid down in bed, I discovered Father's scribbled note. He and my brothers drove to Ferndale, a suburb north of Detroit, to buy Ethiopian food at a shabby, sit-down restaurant owned by my ex-girlfriend's uncle.

Outside I hear the distinctive sound of a donkey begging for dried sugar beets. I bounce out of the bed, bang my foot against a moving box, and twist my neck to look down at the driveway. My hands sweat as I scan the road for Father's car. His car is not downstairs. Another vehicle somehow made that strange sound. I sit down on the bed facing the open window and hold the camera viewfinder up to my eye, trying to see the image in front of me differently. The window like all the windows in my bedroom is painted white and double hung with eight glass cut-ups. White bleeds where the glass connects to wood. On the windowsill, a sun-faded postage stamp is stuck. The eighteen in the upper left corner is barely recognizable. Fathers are like windows. They control how clearly a child sees the world outside. Every time I stare out of my window I see a wedding between a man and woman. It is strange to be reminded of marriage every day, when I want to forget the word. Two years ago, Father told me he had lung disease, and he was afraid what would happen to me when he died.

"When you marry your girlfriend, I'll give you the business," he would often say after that conversation.

I would ask myself if I told him the truth, how long would he wait to do the unthinkable? Somali parents, who find out that their children will not marry due to un-African desires, are expected to set them on fire and spit on the charred ashes and bones.

My bedroom door swings open and my hands jerk. The camera knocks me in the chin. Gray bits stick to the camera's body. I thought I locked the door. In the window's reflection, I watch my little brother's face light up full of wonder. Above his face, Father's face shows the opposite — the taste of bitter expectation.

"Carsten, you missed it," Ricky says.

Father yells over Ricky, "I called the house sixty times. Where were you?"

"I went for a walk," I say to the window.

"Where?"

"To the park, down Southfield Street, and back home."

"How long did it take you?"

"Three hours."

"Three hours," Father says like he does not believe me. "Did you call your girlfriend? Turn around and talk to me."

My lower body feels weighted with industrial concrete. I know I should not obey my father, but if I do not turn around Father will force me to turn around and my punishment will be harsher. I count to four.

Footsteps run. A door slams downstairs. A different door opens somewhere else in the house. And like a tomcat to a kitten, Father snatches me up by the neck, out of bed, into the bathroom to be licked clean. I close my eyes to not remember my face in the mirror, when sleep comes. The jars rattle on the counter as my knees beat the paint-chipped cabinet doors. The slender bottle with the seahorse insignia rolls off the counter, and into a wicker wastebasket. Junior screams stop, however the torture continues. Father's unclipped fingernails feel like blades as I try to free myself.

"Stop," Junior screams.

I stop, and the pain lessens. Father releases my neck. I hear a slapping sound, and then the bathroom door slams closed.

On the other side, Junior bangs and yells, "you bitch."

Nails dig into my neck. The four-petaled faucet molds to Father's all-powerful hand and twists into an accessory. His power, digging into my skin, dunks my head into the deep sink. The water turns pink, swirling and satisfied. Father's hands that are trained to accentuate beauty always uncover ways to change us into strangers. At least underwater I cannot hear him scream.

Chapter 8

The oval-faced business owners at Ford City Mall in West Lawn hated when Father traveled far for photography jobs. Junior and his grubby-fingered friends would terrorize their shops, begging for handouts, or hollering as loud as they could because they could. We were their dizzying sons from the Horn of Africa, privileged, yet poor. My older brother instructed me to walk with at least five people between us at the mall. From afar, I studied my brother like a subject sitting in front of my camera and emulated the hostility he wore under plastic coolness.

The day his friends agreed I acted like him, Junior forced me into a chokehold outside of the discount shoe store. I elbowed him in the gut and received thunderous applause from his howling friends. When Father returned from his two-week gig in Detroit, Junior told him I could take care of myself. Father agreed but slapped Junior for referring to me walaal instead of walaalo. The two long-voiced words are interchangeable as Kodak's Tri-X film with another brand of black and white film – though only one of the words means blood brother. The other word could refer to a female sibling. From that day forward, each time Junior said brother in Somali and then my name, Father punched him. What confused our motherless lives even more was that I often used the word my brother and not my blood brother. Eventually, my older brother stopped speaking Somali, and the space between us thickened, becoming a language of its own. I started haunting my friend's house near the South Loop.

During an oppressive summer afternoon, my friend and I snuck into his older brother's room to steal a kung fu movie. The number of posters with shirtless men and his sexualized comments should have revealed that my friend was testing my straightness. How could I acknowledge or suggest that the maleness of the models aroused my interest over the single buxom diva poster? My friend pushed a videocassette tape into the clunky VCR. The grainy video panned to a wall-hung tool cabinet, to two construction hats, to a mesh jockstrap on a concrete floor, to two nude blonds. The scene mirrored a professional wrestling match, but more provocative. As I gawked with my mouth open, and blood rushed between my thighs, my friend sprinted out of the room, roaring with laughter. The door slammed. That was my golden opportunity to shove the videotape in my underwear and hurry home. The scene switched to two Latinos sitting on a bench in a locker room. One had a neck tattoo and the other played with a dookie rope chain around his neck. At the same time, they stood up. Both wore baggy sweat pants pulled down low, showing stretched out white boxers, then the screen faded black. When the two men reappear, they were naked. I wanted to kiss my friend and experience that, to have on clothes and become naked in my mind and be so unaware of everything except his tongue in my mouth. The title, "Big Booty Boriqua Boyz," then appeared. Unhypnotizing myself from the sex scene, I bolted to the door. My friend tugged on the doorknob. I heard someone yell, *hey*, on the other side, followed by a soft, "ouch" and a louder, "stop punk." The bedroom door swung open. My friend giggled, and I watched the back of his kinky head as he took off to his room. Blood rushed to my tanned face as his brother asked what was in my pocket. The expression on his face softened, and I knew he wanted to ask a personal question, but before he could, I ran out of their house.

Twenty-five minutes later, I stepped off the city bus on North Halsted Street in Boystown. The word adult flashed neon red inside a bookstore window with a gang of men with bright-colored tank tops. The packed store stocked adult magazines and, strangely enough, workout videos, which were cater-cornered to the highly palmed material. At first glance, the workout video covers were equally as erotic as the suggestive magazine covers. However, their back covers were raunchier with Speedos, spandex, short shorts, leotards, string bikinis, underwear, and lighting that transformed the risqué material into see-through deliciousness. *Juan's Butt Blasting Workout*, a homoerotic porn disguised as an exercise video, guaranteed Father would not stomp me to death if found. In contrast, *Honcho* magazine, with an extreme close-up of two hirsute lips kissing, would. I purchased *Juan's Butt Blasting Workout*. Then, returned multiple times and bought *The Chippendales Shakedown, Secrets to Getting Harder*,

Chapter 9

*C*hing, *ching,* the door bells chime and clink as I kick the glass. Clap, I hear in back from Father testing the flash. The front room in the studio is bare and unimpressive. Framed magazine covers, photographs of couples, stacks of bridal magazines, and fresh flowers give it the appearance of a wedding planner's office. The magic hovers behind a floating wall. Step in and the studio space is minimal: white-coated ceiling, high-gloss walls, white infinity cove, and silver equipment cage. Two rows of professional cameras in the cage offer a number of possibilities. I prefer shooting with the Nikons.

At the front counter, I squat low, setting down the case of mangoes, and then jot down a list of equipment to triple-check: camera body, flash units, batteries, filters, and lenses. We have one hour before a photo shoot in the studio. I cross my arms, staring at the dashes. Dashes calm me before and after they get checked off. Tap, tap, I hear, Father's church shoes walking from the back.

"Carsten did you get the. Boy, why are your arms crossed like that?"

I drop them at my side, and huff acknowledging this is my fault. I failed to prepare myself at the door. A son who buys a pair of shoes for his lame father needs to remind himself of his father's disability.

"Why did you keep doing that?"

I stare out of the storefront window to Father's car. It is his second favorite child after my older brother.

"Do you want to be a girl? Girls roll their eyes; boys do not."

"Whatever."

Realizing my mistake, I turn back to him and am unable to move out of the way. He slaps me across the face. I punch him in the chest and watch the life drain from his eyes. He drops to his knees wheezing.

Running around the counter, I yell, "are you okay?" and grab his shoulder.

"Damn you. You little punk," he says and shoves me away. "Get out. Right now." He clutches his chest and squeezes his eyes shut. The lines beside his eyes become pronounced. "Damn you. Damn you." His other hand, a fist, pounds on the floor.

Outside and away from his eyes, I kick a trashcan and the trash spills into the street. Most notable in the heap are mango seeds and junk food wrappers. I feel a loneliness so great that I can see it in the slow movement of the hands of the clock next door. Loneliness is another fear of mine because a lonely person is at home everywhere. My home is with my father. However, the ache for faithfulness within our home lives within me – to have a safe place where I can go as I am and not be questioned. For the first time, I notice the words, Storage Room, painted gold with a black arrow pointing up the stairs beside our studio.

Ching, ching, the door bells chime and clink as I kick the glass, on purpose this time. Forty-five minutes have passed. I grab the pencil off the counter. The wood crunches as I snap it in half. Before I forget, I hide the pieces in my pocket. I should not have hit him. Behind the floating wall, an electric motor whirrs. I step loudly; hear nothing. Then, I walk into the studio into the equipment cage and grab the Nikon I am shooting with today. Father, standing behind his camera, says nothing. We make separate spaces without dividing the room. My mood lightens as I move around the room. Lighting umbrellas, a tungsten light stand, various stands, a ladder, an apple box, and a camera being checked by Father are around the cove. Building the cove took Junior and me two days and painting the ceiling and walls took four. The fumes hurt Father's chest. When he sneezed, and blood blew through his fingers, I asked him to leave and see the doctor again.

The entrance door opens. My palms start to sweat. Father greets the married couple. Heels click on the hardwood. Frankincense wafting from the front reassures me he will not humiliate me. The clients are not Somali.

"Over here," Father directs them to the cove.

"And take off your shoes please," I say. Dirt, from the bottom of shoes, tracks onto the cove, and I have to clean it. Cleaning up takes away from time in the darkroom.

The wife hands their sleeping baby to a wrinkle-faced man that she resembles. The man winks at me while rocking back and forth, kissing the baby. He hums a lullaby in a slow rhythm. The wife twists a lacquer brooch with a maroon background. Blue and orange flowers fill the foreground. A gold braided chain adorns the edge. Her piece appears similar to the ones Russian mothers pin to their breasts in Chicago.

Getting on my knees, I hold up a reflector close to the clients to provide a soft fill light. Father nods at me.

"I came in my best and he wants to be a gigolo. Don't show his hairy man arms."

"I'll try my best."

"I look older than him," the husband says and nods at the wrinkle-faced man. "They're making me a crazy man."

"Isn't he silly?" the wrinkle-faced man says to the baby.

The husband smiles, showing a gold tooth. The two slender men look about the same age; however the husband is dressed younger in a shiny black t-shirt and slacks. The wife wears a black blazer with shoulder pads and a flipped-up collar. The busyness of the top accentuates the smallness of her waistline.

"Carsten, change the lighting."

Experience moves my wrist. I angle the reflector lower to watch the light on them. Father nods again. Our routine is methodical. I assist first; then we switch roles, and I shoot second. We switch again and again until the film runs out.

"Straighten your shoulder," the wife says.

"Don't ever get married, son," the husband says.

"He has to or I will kill him."

Everyone else laughs. I bite my tongue on accident. Clap, the flash goes off. I taste death in my mouth. The door bells ching.

"I will see who it is," I say in pain and run before Father responds.

Behind me, the room glows white from the flash. I pinch my nose to stop the tears, but it does not work. The bells clink as my foot hits the door passing the mailman. Rainwater wets my pants as I run up the stairs and unlock the storage room above the studio. Emptiness greets me like the word, please. I slam the door, and dust falls on my head like snowflakes.

Chapter 10

On every photography job, elegantly packed with cameras and lenses are a mango and pocket knife. Father relishes peeling the flame-colored skin and slicing into the fruit. Then, he cuts thick chunks and inserts the meat into his mouth, using the flat end of the blade. The practice became a sacrament, food as a spiritual service, performed after the final roll of film was finished. Last year, after the wedding of two eighteen-year-olds, their parents insisted we celebrate with them. First, Father savored his mango while joking with the elder men about women and sex, then he asked the bride's mother to prepare our plates. We ate dishes seasoned with cumin, cardamom, cloves, fenugreek seeds, and other spices. The parents and ten elders sat with us in the kitchen and the groom and bride and their guests danced in the living room. Their joy was so alive and contagious that I giggled. Father asked me to join them, but an elder said no, and the decision was final. The man's dead eyes nudged my face refusing to budge. Self-conscious and terrified, I tried to shrink as tiny as possible to the size of a fire ant. A gravelly voiced man whispered a slur, not at me, about a man in a story someone else was telling. The word flew up in the air, buzzing around, seeming less offensive off of his tongue. His skin was pockmarked, scratched, and discolored, a painter's palette of black oils. His ugliness offended me more than the word. The word, ugly too, was not dabbed onto me. So I was thankful. I wanted to wipe the grease off his face, but instead I crept to the banquet table to pour myself a glass of camel milk. Each step, smaller, more particular than the proceeding. Most of the dishes had goat: curry goat, goat stew, goat-filled hand pies, and fragrant rice with goat.

"If there is no meat, it isn't a Somali meal. Eat it all," the one woman said.

Hearing her say that, I felt as finely chopped as the baby goats that had their throats slit earlier that morning.

When I eased into my chair, Father asked, "why do you walk like that," in front of the elders.

"Walk like what?"

"Men do not swish this way and that way."

"I wasn't doing that."

The woman gasped when Father flashed his knife. Her hands covered her eyes, and with the black henna on her hands, they looked like eyes. I dropped my paper plate as I hopped up from my seat. The dead eyes sparkled, waking up from their dream. None of the male mouths moved. Father yelled, *stop*. I bolted out into the living room, past the dancing, out of the bungalow, past the brick homes, and did not stop until I reached the Brown Line on Lincoln Avenue.

A graying man and a teenage girl, both in blue work uniforms, nodded as I boarded the train of my childhood. Amir, his nametag read. Hers read, Maya. She smiled more than the man. I slumped into the seat ahead of them and overheard the man tell the girl, "Yes, he's handsome, but not someone you want to marry." He underlined his you and could have punctuated the end of his sentence with a limp wrist. For Somali elders, fruit always tastes bitter on their tongue.

"What do you mean?" the girl asked.

I squinted over my shoulder, into slices, into the man's eyes, and asked, "Yes, what do you mean?"

My question mark was so sharp-edged, the man snapped his neck to look out of the window, but I did not.

Chapter 11

Lighting to a professional photographer is as provocative as bird's nest jelly to a sous-chef. A built-in flash is lighting at its unsexiest level. Attachments are the definition of sex: strobes, flash meters, hot lights, reflectors, filters, umbrellas, and softboxes. They lead to reproduction – of images, that is. Low lighting can shape a dramatic photo-story; poor lighting, however, can ruin picture quality. In the absence of adequate lighting, even a noted photographer could not produce mediocre work. And, without good lighting I lose focus. The reason I have been in a permanent dazzle staring at Brett for thirty minutes and not memorizing street signs. This Michigan night, a fog-hinted dreaminess, is perfect for woolgathering. High beams passing us on the road cast a shadow of Brett's power over me. Instead of Brett in the driver's seat, I see my father. At intimate moments, Father's image attaches to me like a second body and projects onto the faces of men I find attractive. To detach my father, I allow the camera, strapped around my neck, to become part of my body. The built-in flash will translate a fact to my eyes.

Rocks and rubble thump the truck's underbelly as the wheels screech, turning onto a black path. The truck shakes. My calf smacks against a level and tape measure set on a hook beside the gearshift. Tears come from the shock of pain. Father punched me repeatedly in the same spot yesterday while holding my head down in the sink. A pebble whacks the passenger window, and we slow to a stop. The headlights illuminate the skeleton of a house surrounded by tall trees.

"We won't stay long. I have to make sure they secured the heavy equipment. We've had forklifts and excavators stolen."

"Are we still in Beverly Hills?"

"No, Bloomfield Hills."

The only source of light fades out, and the darkness that settles resembles Somalia at midnight after all whispering campfires have cooled. Brett's door screeches as it opens. Gravel crunches under his gym shoes. The driver door hiccups as it closes softly. A flashlight clicks on, lighting the unpaved footpath to the front door.

Each step that I take in black air is on purpose. Oak swallows the moon. Muted tones and nervousness transform gray-black into the blackest black. My foot kicks a mound and sand sprays into my face. As I struggle, focusing, trying to distinguish shapes, Brett shines the flashlight at my bare legs. I move a quarter step to the left so that the purple bruise on my leg is in shadow. My shirt covers up other injuries. Under the beam, I see a brick and a honeycomb-patterned shoeprint. Trail marks, the width of my feet, lead into the house. We follow the marks inside.

The front door closing creates a sound similar to photographic paper being cut by kitchen scissors. Brett leads the way through the house, and the house slowly reveals itself to us. Eight industrial-size buckets are along the wall that is opposite to the entry wall. The cement floor is unfinished. The walls have a grainy texture. Everywhere light lands the colors live between white and wandering Timberwolf.

Brett eases a rough-textured flashlight into my hand and says, "This is a courtyard."

My flashlight reveals a cold, gray landscape ahead of us.

"We're putting glass sliding doors around here. The living room opens out into four courtyards."

"If you could live in this house with the man you loved, would you?"

"Are you asking to come stay with me?"

"No, I was curious. Somalis are not as accepting as other cultures are. Thinking about telling my father, I am moving in with a man. I feel him choking me."

"But you don't know how he'll react until you tell him."

"That's easy to say."

"Well, if he kicked you out, you could live with me."

"That is not a serious option."

"Why not?" Brett asks.

"Somali families are very different."

"Only if you believe they are."

"They are. Trust me."

"Have you ever had sex with a guy?"

"No. Only oral."

"He approached you, right?"

He liked to throw hunting knives at his bathroom door; it killed time. The slits in the wood were thin enough that quarters could slide through to make a wish. I would rub my frostbitten fingers in the grooves, all smooth, perfect for spying. February is always freezing in the Midwest. Last February, on an exceptionally icy night, he asked about my assignment for *Chicago Magazine* at Union Station. A door slammed as I was finishing my sentence, sitting in the living room. The showerhead squeaked. A curiosity I could not quiet coaxed me off the camelback couch. I peeped into the bathroom through six knife slits, stacked on top of each other like syrupy pancakes, and watched him undress. I loved the roundness of his thick body: the extra skin and the possibility. He bent over grabbing shampoo out from under the cabinet. Him, bending over, made his butt stick out and look rounder. His hand had reached for the doorknob before I had a chance to rush into his bedroom. Naked and ferocious, he yanked me into the bathroom and unzipped my pants. Watching him on his knees confirmed my attraction to men. My eyes locked onto his eyes. Something I could never do with Cecilia. Kissing her was equivalent to sticking my head in a muddy backyard lake to kiss a catfish – delicate and weird. I wondered where to put my hands. My hands fondled every part of his body that I could reach. But something in my friend's face changed, and I saw my father on his knees.

Tonight, Father ate himself to sleep on the couch, devouring a feast of meat, biscuits, cake and pop, allowing me to sneak out the front door. Before I left, I tossed his bloody facial tissues in the kitchen trashcan.

Suddenly, Brett and I are silent and listening. Sounds I could not hear are now blaring: the mechanical rattling of dragonflies, the rapid whistle bursts of crickets, the piercing dziting of katydids, and a two-beat tapping I cannot identify. A shadow passes over my eyes. Maybe a leaf fell or a bird flew over the roof. The night air smells musty; however, the smell might be Brett's underarms. Mustiness is his kiwi and melon. I have the desire to stick my nose in his armpits. My flashlight illuminates his nipples, forearms, and hands. His hands look cut up the way the hands of a man who could kill another man would be. Two long veins run from his right wrist to his forearm and disappear. I hear a faint snorting sound from an animal outside and shine my light in the direction of the noise.

Brett squeezes my free hand, an unfeigned tenderness, superb in its generosity. He slides something small in my hand. The flashlight reveals it is a pocket knife that looks familiar.

"You need to learn how to use this," he says.

Chapter 12

Grunts and quick swipes on wood were constant at Grandfather's house. The basin and crucifix in his front room would vanish throughout the day; however not at the same time. At nine at night, they were returned after guests had left. He bowed to Allah five times a day before coming to America and then identified as Muslim and Catholic. Guest conversations reflected both faiths. *Almsgiving* and *as Allah has willed* were heard after or before *Glory Be, The Rosary*, and *Our Father*. Father learned the Quran and the Bible in Somali, English, and Spanish. As an adult, he buried certain Islamic beliefs he believed interfered with being a photographer. Disgust for dogs was not one of them. Being that dogs leave impurities behind like little treats: urine, fecal matter, sweaty hair, dander, milk, or even worse, saliva. In order to hear God's word, prayer space needs to be pure as a gold banner made of silk. The body needs to be pure as well. He would say, *do not let a mutt come near you. If it touches you, you have to wash that part of the body seven times with river water.*

On the morning that I turned eleven, hearing a knock on our door lit up my face. Father would shake me violently for answering the door. However, I thought it was Grandfather with the camera I wanted. A beer-bellied man was beating on our neighbor's door. An explosive cry from the other side of him jolted me. His Saint Bernard galloped toward us with globs of drool dripping down his mouth. Father screamed. Heavy footsteps hurried toward us, but it was too late. The demon dog leaped up, stood on his hind legs, and licked Father's face. Stinging beads formed under my skin and burst through the skin at my elbows down to my wrists. I saw the globs and itched. The dog stepped with my father, compensating for his unexpected movements, and licked his face clean. Licking his face, he seemed happier than any other dog I had ever seen. The curse words from Father's lips scared me more than the amount of thick drool. When I heard the words, kill, you, and Carsten, I bolted to my bedroom. The first lick of his belt's tongue hit my neck. Gashes and welts covered my chest, legs, back, and arms. A permanent V mark is on my arm from the metal tip.

The next day, a box wrapped in red foil was at the foot of my bed. An oversize card, with I'm sorry written inside, was taped to it. Tissue paper revealed a gorgeous Canon camera with a price tag. Numbers and plus signs whirled in my head, spinning away from me. I knew how much money Father made, our rent, and the amount he gave Grandfather every month. The math did not add up, but we stayed in our place. Now, I own twenty-nine cameras, and five of them are not I'm-sorry-gifts. But who would I be without these cameras?

Still in pain a week later, I quit working with Father. Junior also refused to assist him. He beat us every day until Grandfather called and said the police arrested a friend of Father's. He cleared his calendar. Before the drive, he yelled to dump out our garbage. I found a makeup case in the trash chute room. Black, rectangular, and shiny, it looked and smelled brand new. The light brown face powder glowed inside. Sneaking back inside the apartment, I locked myself in the bathroom and dabbed the puffy sponge on four whiteheads. The hard masses softened, becoming newborn skin. Excited, I dabbed the sponge on the scar on my forehead. My face looked even and smooth.

At the jail, we moved with nervous caution through the series of lonely hallways. The clanks of locking gates did not alarm me. The security check sign leading to a closed room did. A female guard waved us inside with a gloved hand, then searched Junior and Father's front and back pockets.

"Pockets," she said to me three times.

I stared at her stone-faced unable to move or speak.

Father patted my shoulder, whispering, "It's okay."

She smiled pointing to my front pockets and twirled her fingers around for my back pockets. I dropped carrot oatmeal cookies, Russian chocolate, peppermints, my wallet, and change, into the clear bin. After she said thank you and pointed to the door, I heard a camera click outside. The sound confirmed I should be more concerned with being behind a camera than being a beautiful boy. She would have found the case in my back pocket, had she patted me down.

Once inside the visiting room, I ran to the restroom and traced the sign of the cross across my chest. Grunts and moans stopped me at nineteen. On the reflective tile, I made out a man with his face pressed against the wall.

I leaned closer, peaked over inside the next stall through the gap at the end of the divider, and saw another man behind him, pumping his body. The man panted. The wall steamed. The man said, *kiss me*. I squeezed into the corner of the stall, smashing my face against the tile. Some of the bulbs needed replacing, rendering the man into a blur of movement and smudged lips. His skin, even and pale, revealed his young age. He slid his fingers through the opening. The screws that connected the divider to the wall screeched. He pulled it back further. Tattooed on his neck was the word rebel. The men in the stall were both rebels, and I was a co-conspirator. As his breath steamed the tile, I blew on the wall. We shared the same breath until a hand banged on their stall.

"Let us finish," he yelled and they continued.

Feeling dizzy, I rolled my head away from him and covered my mouth to smother the laughter. The sound that came through was like stone being dragged across wood.

Chapter 13

Slipping my finger behind the paper, the book in my lap opens to my babysitter. She has cared for me since I was two. Fifteen years later she is still shield-like, quiet as a snake, and droopy-eyed. The bags under her eyes hang to her teeth. Maybe she is fifty or sixty-five, I do not know. Her mouth has never opened in front of me, but the way she says her name, Dorothy Parker, is as fixed in my head as a tree full of cicadas in the summertime. Her voice is as tattered as her grandmother's wedding dress. Countless nights, I imagined it and made it as sharp as the knife in my hand. I replace the wrinkled newspaper with Brett's pocket knife. The noticeable bulge in between the pages might catch my Father's eye. The last time he found a weapon in his house he broke the person's jaw that hid it. That hammer, hidden among beads, bras, hosiery, and silk scarves serves as a reminder what could happen — a separation.

In spite of that, I am broken with happiness. The knife is a connection; a shape to tessellate Brett and me together, like triangles, so our heads touch. I tilt the book, and the pocket knife slides out, dropping beside my thigh to the bed. When extended, the blade is seven inches in length and three inches in width. The contoured handle, with wood accent, has his initials, B.F., carved into the clear pine. A bar on the knife moves backward and forward into a slot. The motion locks the blade into place. I push the bar gently toward the handle to close the knife and open it again.

The tip halfway covers the word blood on the paper. I stare at the word, in black on newsprint, and an image of meat sellers develops in the darkroom tray of my memory. The print, prodded with tongs, slowly reveals itself. They are sleepy-eyed cutting up lamb and goat and throw the guts on the ground for crying kittens. The street is unpaved and covered with wind-scattered trash. This sandy world is as familiar to me as hearing names like Mohammed, Aasha, Hassan, and Leyla screamed under low sale prices.

I swipe my thumb across the Somali newspaper. The letters E, F, and I become uncovered. I move my thumb more, and the letters N and K appear. *Stabbed, robbed, and left bleeding*, a woman told the reporter. Her statement and others like hers shocked people we know. The knife in my hand will never cut another person – a mango maybe and in secret. I rub my finger over the thin groove of Brett's initials. The etching is perfect, about the same size as my thumbnail. BF sounds like the word boyfriend, but it could also mean best friend.

A glare from the television set reflects on page fifty-two in Avedon's *Portraits*, where Dorothy lives. A men's swimming competition is on; however, I have the volume muted. The cameraman pans to a Somali swimmer stepping onto a slanted starting block. I know his parents are from my grandfather's country by his nose, classic Somali, long and narrow. I have the same nose, inherited from Father. Both my brothers are the same shade of brown as him and have his gaunt face, sharp cheekbones, high forehead, dark brown eyes, and kinky-curly hair. Father calls it the growling stomach look. The swimmer could be someone that we know. Close to Marian on the wall, I hung up a photo-collage of my father and brothers. Looking at my brothers is like looking through family photo albums. I see Father as a boy and a young adult, which is why it is difficult for me to separate him from them. His nose is the only family feature that I inherited. I take after Mother, who is Cuban. I have her tan skin, hazel eyes, and coarse hair. My cheekbones are not as prominent as hers. However, when I smile, close-lipped, my cheeks dimple like Mother.

In the book, the page opposite to Dorothy is stark white and contains a quote by Avedon: "to get a satisfactory print is often more difficult and dangerous than the sitting itself." A child's finger smeared fruit jam under the lustrous words. I retrace my fingers over the red mark. Four of Avedon's later books, my photography guides, are where they usually are, on my bed. Avedon's latest book is on my dresser underneath a Polaroid. A few cameras that Father has given me over the years line the top. They include a Polaroid Land Camera, Graflex Crown Graphic, Pentax K1000, Brownie Bull's-Eye, Leica M6, Ricoh Super Ricohflex, Agfa PD16 Clipper, Nikon F3, and Canon Canonet 28. As well as accessories: Canon battery grip, Nikon flash, manual focus lens, Argus C3 camera, Argus LC-3 meter, Honeywell Tilt-A-Mite flash, and a handle bracket. He gave me *Portraits* after the coldest day of winter in February. I was ten years old, and like a magic trick, the book opened up to Dorothy's face. And, I remembered the first time that I saw her. Her basset-hound eyes reminded me of a comedic cartoon character. A noise between a dog's bark and the whoo of an owl came out of my mouth. As I look out of my window at everything green, it is impossible to believe that Chicago and Beverly Hills are freezing in February up until May.

The doorbell chimes twice downstairs. At the front door, the face staring at me scares me because Father will pull up at any minute.

"I almost didn't recognize you. Without your face behind your chuh chuh," Brett says. He transforms his hands into a rectangle and presses down on an imaginary shutter button.

"What are you doing here?"

"Your dad mentioned to my dad. There's a leak in your basement. I came to check it out."

"Did my father tell you to stop by?"

"No, he didn't ask me to."

Before I can think of a lie for him to leave, Brett drags his work boots on the knobby doormat. The leather tool belt around his sinewy waist has an attachment with multiple pockets. A messenger bag, covered in light-colored nicks, hangs over his shoulder. He swings the bag back behind him. His work uniform, a dingy white t-shirt, and paint-stained jeans, fit tight against his body. I stare at fresh, fingernail-size cuts on his forehead. On his neck and the top of his shirt, there are dried dots of what looks like cement. His mustache is thicker than it was yesterday, and his beard has grown in light but covers his lower jaw area and neck. His face looks tanned, slender, and slightly more masculine. The heaviest door closes me in and my body tenses, listening out for Father.

As he scratches his back, walking into the kitchen, Brett asks, "Where is everyone?"

"I'm the only one here."

His blue jeans sag revealing the top of his fleshy bottom. His skin down there is smooth and buttery. I could slip my hand in his pocket and yank his jeans to his knees, but I can't; Father could be outside. My hands sweat. His skin color lightens under the harsh kitchen lights.

Brett steps one foot at a time down the concrete stairs into the dank smelling basement. Our basement resembles a bomb shelter from the slabs of concrete. No signs of life exist here, except spider webs. I find myself fixated, staring at the curve of his backside. Then, I notice his work boots. The boots are the same color as two rampant leopards with hungry tongues on the Somali coat of arms. The spotted animals support the light blue shield that has a white star in the center. The shield is the same color as the Somali flag. Below the shield, a golden ribbon drapes itself around two crossed spears and two crossed palm fronds. Everything for me floats back to my grandfather's country. And, back to practicing formal worship as a child, while wearing a Patron Saint Christopher pendant. Father nearly decapitated me tucking the necklace under my shirt the second he saw it. My upbringing has wedged me between rosary beads and Islamic prayer beads; and azuki beans mixed with butter and sugar on Monday and black beans and rice on Friday. And, I am stuck between his expectation of who I should be and my fear of who I am. However, every time I convince myself he is to blame for me feeling stuck, I cannot explain why not telling him I like men is easier than telling him and dealing with whatever happens.

At the bottom of the stairs, Brett asks, "Besides photography, do you have any other talents I should know about."

"None I can share with a neighbor."

"Tell me now or I'll push you to the ground and bounce on you until you do."

"Just kidding."

"I'm not."

We laugh at the joke and then, neither of us knows what to do; at least I assume he does not know because I am unsure. I shove my hands in my pocket, and he copies me. After a while, he steps closer, so close that the space between us prepares to collapse. I walk around him to hold onto the moment longer. A change occurs in the room, and we do not acknowledge either's excitement. But it is there between our legs. Hiding it is unnecessary at this point.

Yanking my shirt out of my pants, Brett laughs, and says, "please keep it out."

Polo shirts, creased khakis, sometimes rolled up at the bottom, and brown loafers, are my everyday uniform, schoolboy realness, real enough to blend in. "You need to loosen up a little. Did I offend you?" He opens his arms out to cling to this moment longer. Both of his arms wrap around me, pressing my chest into his chest. It is an embrace between two men comfortable with their closeness and trying to become even closer. Our lips almost touch as his face slides across mine as we separate.

"Look up there," he says, standing under the stairs. "There's a crack,"

The crack that he points to is a pencil-thin line, the length of the moving truck Father rented.

"It's causing some buildup. I can tell your dad I can start tomorrow."

"Don't. Let me," I say while constructing a lie to get out of shooting the wedding booked in Detroit tomorrow night.

Chapter 14

Daredevil cliff divers lured tourists away from Europe to Acapulco in the 70's. Young men in Speedos stretched out their arms to swan dive off a dizzying cliff plunging into shallow water. They transformed into acrobatic fish-eating birds. Wide-eyed onlookers held their breaths. A divers' miscalculation meant life or death. For the divers, it was freeing, seeing the world from above; the way seabirds view the world. It was dream-like. They awoke underwater; that is how one local described it.

Two years ago, in 1996, Father snatched up an assignment shooting a festival in the city of dreams for the Chicago Tribune. He arranged that I would receive one hundred dollars to photograph five up-and-coming singers from Mexico City. On the second day, I asked Father if I could shoot the cliff-side performance while he shot a jazz band from Cape Verde. He told me to wait, without screaming, and after he finished, we could hike to the cliff together. Hours earlier, I met a loudmouthed boy my age with perfect eyebrows at the café next to our hotel. He was drinking coffee and smoking cigarettes with a group of young men in Speedos, of all ages and all with white teeth. I sat down at the table beside theirs, and he sat in the chair in front of me. He pronounced my name "Car-Seat." In English, he asked if I could photograph him diving. Through my limited Spanish, I said of course and asked him to pose standing in front of the coffee shop. I shot a provocative picture of him, from the shoulder up, looking into the camera with a lit cigarette in his mouth. His face was sexual and beyond sexual in front of the red-painted sign. He smoked cigarettes, not like chain smokers on the street do during winter in Chicago. He smoked slow and deliberate like he was savoring a decadent dessert. Or, maybe he was attempting to memorize the taste of the ceremony. Then, I shot him in profile highlighting the trail of peach fuzz leading into his red Speedo.

For me, it was dream-like watching him fly off the August-colored cliff. The cliff looked sculpted with rust, tangerine, and beige clay. His muscular body turned into a tumbling rock and then turned weightless in the salty air. The seconds after he dissolved in the foaming Pacific and emerged unscratched seemed like hours.

After he had strutted back up, we carried on a colorful conversation without words. We stood about twenty feet away from each other and used our heads, hands, and lower bodies. I hid behind Father preventing him from seeing us speak. While gesturing I could not leave, I kicked over Father's drink at my feet. He knocked me across the face. My camera dropped to the ground. The cracking sound ripped up my insides. I stared at the broken telephoto lens and without thinking I punched Father in the face. He fell, and his head crunched on impact. He did not move. Neither did anyone else around us.

The diver helped me move him away from the gawking crowd to a grass-covered area. "Look at his chest rising. You didn't kill him," he said.

"He will kill me the second he wakes up."

"When he opens his eyes give him more to drink. He won't remember anything."

The diver waved down the shirtless vendor, selling Mezcal in an ice cream cart, and bought two. When father woke up, I told him to drink to feel better, and he guzzled down both. The pulpy mix was dark red and tasted as if it had strawberry, pineapple, coconut, cream, and sugar. Later, a balding hotel employee told me the drinks sold on the cliff were alcoholic, and I should not drink them. The alcohol in my two cups was tasteless. The drink I spilled was Father's second as well. The diver waited with me, rubbing my back and offering me cigarettes until my brothers found us. I told them that Father fainted from the heat. Father came to, and my younger brother asked him, what happened.

"I do not know," Father said, stuttering.

Junior laughed.

Knowing I could start laughing, I faced the tanned men on the cliff, exposing my excitement only to them. Junior draped Father's hairy arm around his sweaty shoulder and said he would walk him to the hotel and that I should continue photographing the performance. The moment my Father and brother's heads vanished from the rock path, the diver pulled my hand. We sprinted down a different path with lush vegetation, through a palm tree forest, out to a beach blanketed with naked men. The diver slid down his Speedos. I peeled off my sticky t-shirt. His tongue forced its way into my mouth. His body was as stiff as the howling wind by the cliffside. We stood on the golden beach, barefoot, dancing, kissing and groping each other until we heard a baritone laugh. Beside us, a bush-bearded woman in a pink sequin gown whistled. We laughed, running behind a rock. He rolled down my swim trunks. Joined together in want, we lowered to the sand and connected genitally and sensually and fell asleep. Footsteps woke us. I rushed back to the hotel, shirtless, with my hands in my shorts, hiding my erection.

The key grinding sound in our room lock should have reminded me who I was. At the door, Father slammed his forehead against my forehead and grimaced with blood-shot eyes.

"I could choke you right now," Father screamed. "What happened to your camera?"

"You broke it."

When his hand rose, I saw his face under better lighting.

Not only had the Mexican sun given him an even tan, but also, I had given him a black eye. Father seeing the black eye meant life or death for me. I fed him red-colored drinks during the remainder of the trip.

Chapter 15

Walking inside, whiffs of cooked goat, roasted cauliflower, garlic, chilies, and lemon assure me we're in the right place. The sign outside only says Shorty's. Reddish-brown, yellowish-brown, brown, and green herbs in barrels emit scents of a Somali kitchen. Rice crunches under my gym shoes. Snap, pause, snap, fingers create a beat in a song playing. A man in one of the aisles hums along. Further inside the market, I smell onions, burnt matches, frankincense, curry, and floral black tea. Camel milk, goat milk, sheep milk, buttermilk, and fruit juice bottles line the refrigerated cases. A prepared food counter, with hot lights, glows in the back. The pale blue walls contrast with the golds, oranges, limes, and pinks on the shelves from fabrics, packaging, tins, and trinkets. Dozens of white stars adorn the walls. Each is five-pointed and perfect. On the sidewall, Somali proverbs have been painted in large letters. The word "women" capitalized stands out in one, and it reads, *Where there are no WOMEN, there is no home.* Underneath it, is the proverb, *Get to know me before you reject me.* A buffalo's tongue, in an advertisement, underlines the last two words.

"Salam alaikum," Father says to an older man.

"Thank you, son," the man says and repeats the greeting. He unhooks a pink box, hands me a slice of cake in a lace doily, then gives Father a slice.

The cake is three-layered with white frosting and white filling. I taste cinnamon, cardamom, ginger, vanilla, coconut, raisins, orange, carrots, and a woman laughing. An oil smudge stains the doily.

"My son you want another, no?"

The man hands me a second slice.

Before I can say thanks, Father says, "You are too kind to us, uncle."

A flash of pink at the end of the aisle disappears over to the next aisle as I lick my fingers. The pink is a collarless, pullover shirt worn by a young Somali man. Through the shiny material, I see his pierced nipples. His features are mousy, and his ears stick out on his small head. He dyed his short curly hair blond. His goatee and the patch of hair under his lower lip match. Strands of gold chains loop around his neck in a gaudy fashion. They vary in length with the longest reaching below his belted waist. Gold rings exaggerate the length of his neck. On his wrists, he wears gold cuff bracelets. His pants are a darker pink and have a gorgeous floral print. The belt is black; however the print is floral. Dark eye shadow and pencil highlight his hazel eyes. Every eye in the back of the market follows him.

"What the hell," the server at the food counter says.

"Khaniis," the older man says.

Father repeats the slur, then says, "twelve," to the server, pointing at the sambusas under the hot light. The man ignores them as he flips over a bag of corn flour. A yellow mist falls from the bag. My palms start to sweat. I tap my chest feeling for my camera, on a strap around my neck, and touch nothing. It's in the car, I remember. The server's eyes do not move from the man's direction as he boxes the puff pastries along with mango chutney and fava bean salad. Following behind Father, I grab a container of caramel fudge with camel milk and cardamom. The man slinks past the tea, coffee, and dessert aisle to the next aisle in the back. Father huffs, dropping the take-out boxes on the front counter. I push the candies behind it and search for the man with the gold chain strands, but don't see him.

A minute later, the cashier mumbles, "khaniis," looking in my direction.

"What's the problem?" someone says.

The man with the gold chain strands stands behind me in line.

"You're the problem. Get away from my son."

Father yanks me behind him. My elbow bangs against something flat and hard and throbs in pain.

He hawks up phlegm, spits in the man's face, and slaps two twenties on the counter, stomping to the exit.

Looking over my shoulder, I watch as the man wipes the gob of spit from his cheek. He hands the cashier a single bill, but he throws his hands above his head.

"Get to know me before you reject me," the man says.

Hearing that, I know I can be as strong as him. Strength is being honest in the face of death. It outlasts death. The world outside of the glass door comes alive with newness. The hinges groan as I open it.

Chapter 16

A matte black bible with thick gold lettering is one of the few possessions I have of my mothers. On the first page is the hand-written message, *He who tells the truth doesn't sin but causes inconvenience, love Fatima Tynes.* My grandmother, Fatima Tynes was my mother's babysitter from age two to thirteen. At age two, I learned that honesty could lead to violence. How I learned, is one of Father's gift-wrapped stories to present to the family, gathered, eating dinner during the holidays. He starts the humiliating story snapping his fingers, a Somali gesture meaning long ago, then he says, "The first time I spanked Carsten," in his storytelling voice.

And the story goes:

While reading a magazine alone in his bedroom, Father heard a crashing sound in the winter morning chill of our apartment.

Next Father says, "Before checking in on you boys, I glanced into the guest bathroom."

He noticed a dark flat object smaller than his hand on the tiled floor. When he flicked the light switch, he saw the tip of another object sticking out of the toilet bowl. Submerged in the water was his prized Diana camera. The same cheap, boxy camera he used shooting soft dream-like pictures that his editor at the Chicago Tribune said made him breathless. Part of the back of the camera had broken off. The tube-shaped lens barrel, black on the inside, had broken off as well. Bits of pale blue pieces and black pieces, from the plastic camera, had settled in the bottom of the toilet.

Junior loved sneaking into Father's bedroom, stealing his cameras, and pretending to be a wild animal photographer in Africa. Naturally, Father thought Junior destroyed the camera. He busted into Junior's room. Junior was snoring in bed and by default exposed me as the wrongdoer. To me, Father's cameras were Triple X-rated, forbidden, and shiny toys to fondle.

"The naughty boy wasn't asleep in his bed," Father says, retelling the story.

Father flipped up the lid to the wicker clothes hamper that I enjoyed eating animal crackers inside. Then, he flung open the doors to my sliding closet. Six wood slats fell. A cheaply churned out product, the two doors were entirely horizontal slats, from the top to the bottom. The slats fell with the tiniest tap.

"You weren't hiding under the bed either," Father says.

Rage transformed Father into Grandfather, and he hurried into the kitchen, flinging open the bottom cabinet beside the refrigerator that was free of pots and pans and Tupperware and cleaning products. Two frightened eyes widened. He dragged me out, helpless, crying, and kicking.

"Did you move my camera?" Father yells in character. "Wee did it. You whined."

Wee is how I pronounced Reed, what my older brother prefers people to call him instead of Junior.

"Don't ever move my cameras again," Father yells.

He smashed my head down on the kitchen floor, forgetting I was his child, and not a rag doll made of cloth. Repeatedly, he punched my face and neck until the high-pitched barks of the dog in the apartment below ours un-hypnotized him, and he was no longer his father beating himself as a boy. After the spanking, as Father refers to it, I crawled under my bed. I screamed and pounded my fists, breaking the pain. Father locked himself in his bathroom on the opposite side of the apartment where he could not hear the screaming.

"I was miserable for the rest of the day," Father says.

And the way that he says, "I'm sorry," next, for what happened fifteen years ago, leads me to believe he is apologizing for every time he knocked my head to the floor after that. I need to believe that.

When Father was younger, Grandfather would pummel him until his knuckles were bloody. Father told him that he would never beat his children when he became a father. With his first-born son, Reed Junior, I guess it felt natural, the first punch. The sound probably carried him back to his childhood, like the hoot of an owl, mixed with fruit bats fluttering over a mud hut. Fist to bone. Lesson to the flesh. Never forget son that you are mine.

Chapter 17

Since childhood, I have believed memory is a string of beads that can be restrung and worn again. Like right now, while laughing and speeding, I know I have seen this street before, from this view, in this car. However, I feel more present and aware. I feel the way a shark feels at a card table, seconds before seeing which card will be flipped over. I take in and hold onto the colors and the sounds and the shock on Brett's face. He stomps on an imaginary brake pedal in the passenger seat while squeezing the assist grip. A bead, once cloudy, shines around my head. As I press the window switch up, the smell of alcohol spreads through the car. A chemical must have spilled in the back, but I cannot identify the smell. Through the rearview mirror, I see Father's jacket, his necktie, a crate of mangoes, a paper bag, junk food wrappers, yesterday's newspaper, and a flash case on the back seat. Whatever spilled is on the floor. Blue lights blink behind us. I try not to notice them. Brett rolls up his window, and I crack the two in the back. The scent unfolds as if it is under my nose. With the police car closer, I brake and push the gas to not look guilty.

"Fuck. We're going to jail," Brett says and crosses his arms. His nipples poke out of his mesh tank top.

I glance at the street, then in the back seat. An object glints under father's jacket. As I stare at it, it resembles a glass bottle. The officer speeds up and is directly behind me. I signal and turn onto a street with buildings the color of faded ladybugs that have wide mouths and stairs for tongues. The police car's tires screech as it tears off down the main street.

"Thank, God."

"Do you smell that?"

"Do you realize how lucky we are?"

"Of course, I do."

Reaching over into the backseat, I search the floor but find it empty. I push the jacket over and see the object that shined is the seat belt buckle. On the crate, I notice a clump of pulp and splattered juice stains. I tip the crate, and something slimy touches my hand. A fuzzy spot with gray patches covers the mango. The other fruits have brown and black lesions.

"We can turn back now," Brett says.

"Why? We are not even close yet."

"Are you sure you still want to do this?"

"Yes."

"What if your dad wakes up and sees his car is missing?"

"I want him to so he will see it's missing."

"This isn't like you."

"You told me to stand up for myself. I'm standing up."

"No, this is car jacking. We could get arrested for this. If we do, you won't have to worry about your dad killing you. Because I'll kill you." He pinches my nipple, and I slap his chest and pull on his nipple. "Where are we going?"

"Downtown Detroit."

"Where in downtown?"

"No particular place."

"We can drive to Woodward. The street the museum is on. And, walk around Midtown."

"Can you show me the way there?"

The world glows golden orange from the street lights in Midtown. As we walk in silence, the lighting illuminates Brett, changing his skin gold. His orange shorts disappear under the lights, creating a nude illusion. His legs are one thick muscle. I shave off a sliver of sweet mango, using his pocket knife, and hand it to him. I cut a thin piece for myself too. My hands are sticky with juice and saliva. I imagine the fruit is golden, and by eating it we glow like Detroit. Pretending is a valuable tool for a photographer. He has to transform himself and the subject in front of his camera by giving it an invented life. I slice off a bigger piece for Brett.

He holds half of it out of his mouth and says, "Bite it."

Juice bursts in my mouth and down my mouth to my neck.

A group of younger kids wearing hooded sweatshirts and bookbags drag their feet toward us. One straddles a bicycle and is out ahead of the group. He rocks his head side-to-side and in quick jerks as if listening to a hammering hip-hop beat. One blows out smoke and passes marijuana to the next kid. Another leans his head back, coughs loudly, and sends a bottle of alcohol in the opposite direction. From their height, they could be twelve, thirteen, or fourteen, but no older than sixteen. In the light, their faces are all teeth, acne, anger, and disconnectedness. Childhood is a black-blue midnight, opaque and full of sorrow. The one ahead of the others laughs, and then the rest of the boys follow.

"Look at the girls," the leader shouts with his hands in his pockets.

"Girls, girls, girls," the boys rattle off, becoming louder until it sounds as if they are surrounding us. However, they are surrounding us, a gang of them, maybe nine. They move in locking us in the middle. A bookbag unzips behind me. A lighter flicks. One of them hacks up phlegm and spits. One of them throws his bag on the sidewalk.

"Girls shouldn't be out at night," the leader shouts.

"Girls shouldn't be out at night," the other boys say together.

The leader's hood drops, and I see my father's face on his shoulders, then I realize he is Somali. His buzz cut shows two C-shaped keloids on both sides of his head. They resemble the curved horns of mountainside goats in Ethiopia. A similar mark, but smaller, is on his cheek. The marks, perfect and symmetrical, seem pressed into his flesh with a branding iron. He grins, lights something in his hands on fire, and throws it at our feet. Pop, pop, the firecracker explodes. Pop, pop, another goes off behind my foot. Smoke. Sparks. Panic. Cigarette lighters glow in each kid's hand. A street light above us flickers and turns off. Their faces darken in their hoods. Smoke from the firecrackers and marijuana mix making me feel lightheaded. Then, the ground glows orange from all of the firecrackers exploding. Sounds fade out, the kids move in, and the closeness silences the city.

Chapter 18

Under the razor-sharp rage, it is not difficult to detect a boyish softness. His hatred is seated in his gut, stirring in his bowels, and dictating what drops out of his mouth. The city has a way devouring the young and spitting them back out to devour others. I grew up with boys like him, who have become part of the cement at street corners. With their eyes always watching and their hands always wanting something that does not belong to them. These boys are their younger brothers. The words I hear the leader scream do not match the rage in his hands. The muffled sound in my ear changes to ringing, and then the words become language.

"Give me your cash, bitch," the leader shouts.

"I'm not giving you a damn thing," Brett yells.

The leader pokes out something from the inside of his pocket, like a gun, and says, "You wanna die tonight, bitch."

Knowing the object is his hand, I hurl the mango at his head and his back slams on the sidewalk. I rush toward him, stabbing the air with the knife. The kids scurry in every direction like rats on train tracks.

"No. Stop it, man. Damn. We were just playing," the leader shouts. He crawls from under the metal holding him down.

From behind us, one of the boys throws the glass bottle, and it crashes beside my foot. Alcohol splashes on my legs. I turn and the leader runs off. As he runs and the other boys too, I see the children that they used to be running along beside them. The leader swings his head around. His eyes, almond-shaped, large, and expressive, flood with fear.

"Little boys shouldn't be out at night, bitch," Brett yells after him.

"No, they should not," I yell.

Brett crosses his arms, bends over, and laughs so loud a flock of pigeons fly out of the tree nearby. While staring at the shards, everything pressing against my head feels as if it is a matter of life or death. Underneath the glass, ants rush away from me. I pick up a large piece and see myself through its lens with the knife.

As I shove his knife into my pocket, Brett says, "if you can save my life, you can save yourself."

I hold onto the words and press them down into memory like baby's breath in a Bible. Even when its pages yellow and crumble, I will remember the quote. Dried flower flakes, pressing against the letters, might create brand new words. The meaning will still be the same, however. All around us, the street lights lose their allure. I need to rub something with my hands, but my camera is in father's trunk. A camera would highlight Brett's lower body and the lines behind him, the way his body is darkly lit.

"Brett, let's head back."

"We should. This city is too dangerous for us."

"I hope he comes back for his bicycle."

"We should wait on the other side of that car and jump out at him."

"He might pee in his pants."

"I want to do this again. Next time we should drive my truck."

"No, I want to take my father's car again."

"I won't get in next time."

"Yes, you will. I'll make you."

"We'll see about that."

Sitting down in the driver's seat is like lighting a firecracker. A flame explodes the mangoes and instead of smoke, my lungs fill with sugar alcohol. The scent changed as if someone burnt matches to disguise the smell. I lower my window; Brett taps on his. On the utility pole beside the car, someone stapled a flyer that says, "Are you looking for a Photographer?" with pictures crowding the top and tear strips at the bottom. Only two tear strips are left. Photographers are not as visible in Detroit as they are in Chicago. Chicago grows photographers from the icy ground like they are a national product. Walking downtown, I had to be careful, or I would trip over camera bags or tripods or squatting photographers every few feet. Junk food wrappers rustle under Brett's feet. I reach for the radio knob, but stop, hearing a soft snapping sound.

"Damn. We are almost out of gas. Is there a gas station close by, Brett?"

"There has to be one on this street. How long do we have?"

"Three miles. Maybe four."

"That's enough."

The snap sounds again, and the car spits and sputters and slows to a stop in the street while my foot is on the gas pedal.

"No, no, no, no," I say and punch my leg.

"Does your dad have a gas can in the car?"

"No."

"Let's push the car into that spot and walk to a station."

Hearing the word push, heaviness tightens my chest. A shirtless man, who looks out of place, speed walks past my window wearing short running shorts. The three neon stripes flash. From the side slit in his shorts, I see the curving line of his white briefs. His underwear is as pale as his skin.

Hopping out of my seat, I yell, "Excuse me. Do you know where the closest gas station is?"

He turns around, jogging in place, and adjusts himself between his legs. "Yes. Further up. By Clay Street."

"How far is that?"

"About a ten-minute ride."

"Thank you."

"Thanks," Brett says, leaning on my shoulder.

The runner slaps his thighs in a wave motion as he jogs off down the empty street.

Brett strokes my chest in a circular motion, and I hope the stroking does not end.

"Let's start walking now. We can buy a gas can, fill it up, and hurry back. Your dad won't even know it happened."

"This was a stupid idea. I don't know what I was thinking."

"So! We ran out of gas. It doesn't make this stupid."

"No, I only have four dollars in my pocket. Do you have cash?"

"I forgot my wallet at home."

"I can't believe this. My father is going to kill me."

"Kidding. I have enough."

I pinch Brett's nipple through his shirt, and he slaps my chest and pulls on my nipple.

"Let's grab some mangoes too. If someone else tries to rob us, we can beat them with fruit."

I laugh, and cannot stop, and have to sit down in the car from how much my back hurts from laughing.

"Let me get my camera out. You have to pose with a mango."

"Why?"

"Fruit with a fruit."

Chapter 19

The lights flicker providing a slow reveal. Camel brown becomes cream and cream becomes milk. As I stare at Brett, stare around in wonder, time slips out of my hands and away from me into the whiteness. Its pull transforms us into moths, and we dance around the room in an endless spiral. Without the equipment cage, I might believe we entered through the door and slipped inside of a light bulb. The walls look so luminous that they seem made with slabs of artificial light. The walls, cove, and ceiling are Wedding Dress White, the name on the paint can. A white whiter than the other swatches at the hardware store: Bright White, Green Glaze, Twinkling Crystal, White Yarn, Apple Blossoms. I picked the color, not because of the name, because of its promise. Courage does not come to a man overnight, and neither does a woman in a wedding dress. It promised development. It promised newness. The choice made me feel ripe and clear. Brett's voice squeals with excitement like someone much younger, more observant, and untouched by the hurt of the adult world. I hear his voice, but not the words, too soft to detect. Then, I see five number fives in a list I taped on the wall. Five, I press it into my palm like a rosary. Four thirty-one, the wall clock shows, and now we have four minutes before it is time to leave. As I arrange our shoes in a neat row, his pink socks bounce into the darkroom. In the darkroom, chemicals muddle the scent of frankincense, but the scent pokes its head through the vinegary veil. I am made of everything that is in this room: air, water, wood, and metal.

"What's the first thing you do when you walk in here?"

"Put on my goggles, apron, and gloves."

"Where are they? I want to feel like you."

The goggle strap licks his curls and shocks his hair, then the gloves snap. I unhook the apron from the coat rack, step behind him, and drape it over his warmth. While tying the strings in back, I catch my Father's eyes. My hand brushes Brett's backside. The act, accidental and small, feels deliberate and vulgar. I fill the space between our bodies with distance and vinegar but lean my nose closer. Must and frankincense blend in the air around Brett's neck. The urge in between my legs pulses and is sticky, but I force myself into stillness. The stillness is a precaution. Father's eyes watch us from the wall as if he is the patron saint of dead insects. Under his holiness, we are lowered into ants under his bronzed feet. Under the lights, his face shines like the sun in full power at midday. Those eyes are like heavy hands squeezing air from my lungs until his hands replace them. I cut my eyes at the redness, at the root, at the reach, and my hips jerk. Brett's face, a mirror of my body, reddens and rises.

"Put on your dad's apron. What do you do next?"

"Prep everything."

"So this is what being in a darkroom feels like for you. It's not what I imagined.

"You get use to the closeted feeling."

"No, this weighs a lot," he says, shaking the apron. "And it's not dark."

"We turn off the lights when we develop film."

"How do you do it? Being in here with him for hours."

"When we're in here. There's a love between us that goes beyond being a father and son. We are equals. It's only when we leave the darkroom that I worry."

"Imagine what you could do if you told your dad you're in love with me."

"I would have more time to beat up kids and steal their lunch money. Because I would be homeless."

A squeaking sound, at first faint, then louder, multiples into desperation. The sound is as infrequent as the sound of my older brother's voice in the studio, but I could recognize both blindfolded and in the dark.

"You hear that," Brett says, staring at the ceiling, in a way that suggests whatever it is might fall.

"There are rat traps in the storage room upstairs. It's a rat trying to escape. These buildings downtown are old; they remind me of home."

Above our heads, Father crept and set the cheese trap for the rats, a Polaroid trap for Junior, and a female trap for me. Junior's trap and my trap switched around years ago in Chicago.

"Were there any more good mangoes?"

"There was only one."

"I'm hungry."

"I'll take you home."

"That'll make me feel better. I keep thinking your dad's going to wake up and go ballistic."

"It wouldn't be new."

With the keys clattering at the door, our downtown seems smudged by practicalness. Even the glow from the lampposts looks sterile, far from the dreaminess of Detroit's golden lights. Brett's shoulder bone looks as pointed as the blade of a pocket knife through the glass. As the fourth lock clicks, something smacks the side of my face. Brett grins over my shoulder and in the glass, Father's goggles and apron float in front of my body like cutout clothing over a paper doll.

"Don't become him, please," Brett says.

"I am him."

"Are you going to wear it home?"

"I'll bring it back tomorrow."

One, two, three beeps, and the security alarm activates inside the studio. In one movement, I wipe my finger across his nipples, force my finger inside a mesh opening, hook him, and force him off of the sidewalk, into the street.

"Where are we going?"

"The convenience store. I'll buy you anything under three dollars."

After walking from the gas station and then turning onto the expressway without speaking, I drove here to untie our tongues. The convenience store is another set of cones in the road.

"Wait, I have to pee. Do you have a bathroom at the studio?"

"Yes."

"Damn, those locks. Come with me first."

Running past smoke and a conversation in Arabic, into the alley, he drops my hand and runs ahead of me to the dumpster. I step over the puddle, beside him, and pee too on beetles, cigarette butts, pizza crusts, and chicken bones.

"Remember when you said I should tell my father that I love you. I do love you. I love you this much," I say and aim for Brett's bare leg.

His leg jerks from the splash of urine.

"You fucker," he screams, trying to grab me, missing the apron and my arm.

But I'm already finished, gliding like a moth to the street light above the car. While laughing so hard, that Father's goggles pinch the side of my face. The feeling is a snap, tiny, yet painful. The pinching proves that courage is uncertainty.

Chapter 20

Giddy from getting away with it, I run into the street roaring. Hands behind me. Lips over teeth. I eat the night, gulping it down, and taste salt. Eagerly, without caring who sees, I choke on the bones. The wind cools my face, but I'm faster than the wind. I eat more, wiping sweat and spit from around my bottom lip. And I eat until my jaw hurts, and I laugh at how my jaw hurts. Father's darkened bedroom pronounces he is dreaming. *Shhh*, Brett whispers, running behind me. Whispering turns to pleading then chasing. I chase him to his house next door. His garage, an open sore, hides nothing but secrets and signals. Colors change. Objects silver under the moonlight. A pile of silver clangs as my leg hits it. I feel the sharpness before I know what is causing it. When I see it sticking out, I squeeze my fists, arms, and chest until my entire body becomes a cowry shell. Hopping on my other leg, Brett helps me to the wall onto the floor. If pain exposes the amount of danger someone is in, the blood trickling down my leg indicates I should run home. However, across the garage, Brett's face in a mirror promises me that the pain isn't a sign. No matter how much of my blood that I wipe away, I tell myself, *stay*. Then, a chill in the air opens my eyes, and I catch the back of Brett running into his house. Without his face to calm me, I tighten every part of my body to feel the contraction of muscles and not the burning. A tap on the top of my foot relaxes my calves.

Unrolling my sock, he presses a dressing to the wound. The sting of alcohol lessens as I hear his breath in my ear. The flatness of the ceiling is off. Even the gasoline smell is wrong, but the heat on my neck corrects their failure. The pipe, the cause of my pain, points toward the street with a triangular tip. The tip is busted, ridged, and resembles a Christmas tree. It stabbed me halfway between my ankle and knee.

"I stole my Father's car, was attacked by kids with firecrackers, ran out of gas, and ran into a pipe."

"And don't forget, peed on my leg."

"And peed on your leg. I have a question to ask you. Is this still the best night ever?"

"Tonight still is the best night ever. Your dad doesn't know we stole his car. Let me walk you upstairs to your room."

"To the front door."

"To the stairs."

"To the stairs. Not up the stairs. Some of the steps creek."

Bending my leg to stand shoots sharp shards throughout my body. I tighten up, saying, *"motherfu."* The ending is torn off with teeth. I bite down on my lip, pounding the floor. "I can't stand up. It hurts."

"I have blankets in my room. We can lay down out here for a while."

"That's a good idea."

I blink, and he is shirtless. Brett balls up his shirt and places it into my palm.

"Squeeze it until I get back." From a box beside us, he finds a hooded sweatshirt. "Put this on. It's cold out here. Can I ask you a question? Why don't you ever talk about your mother?"

"It reminds me how far away she is."

"Where does she live?"

"Cuba."

"Why does she live there?"

"She was deported," I say and drop the shirt, drawing a line between us on the floor.

"Do you have anything of hers?"

I nod.

"What?"

After minutes of silence, I say, "Her wedding ring."

"Let her be the source of your strength. I'll get the blankets."

Like his shirt, I crumple on the floor. Without something in my hand to crush, I feel around and touch something cold, circular, and lightweight. A paint can, I see when I raise my head. The front door opens then I smell cigarette smoke. Smoke and whistling float into the garage. The whistling stops, then I hear footsteps on the pathway. Fighting the pain, I force myself up to my feet.

"Who's that?" someone asks as I'm hopping toward the door into the house. The male voice is unfamiliar. I hear a thud, something like a glass bottle placed on the floor. "Who's that?" the man asks again.

From his build, I know he isn't Brett's father; however, I cannot make out the details of his face because of his camouflage cap. A blond beard and the cigarette hide the shape of his lips. The moon lights his chest and the hairs on his stomach as well as the bush sprouting up from under his sweatpants. The man spits out the cigarette and rushes me, tackling me to the ground. His knee bumps the bandage. I moan from the feeling, a spreading unbearableness. His hands clamp down around my wrists, stretching my arms out to the side.

"Call the police. He was trying to break in," the man says.

"Stop! It's Carsten," Brett yells.

"Your friend," the man says, snapping back. Both their hands help me to stand. "I'm sorry. I saw the hoodie and knew you weren't Brett. Sorry. And you're bleeding. Did I cut you?"

"He ran into a pipe over there. The bandage came off when you were trying to grope him. Carsten, this is my uncle."

"I don't usually body slam friends of the family like that. That hurts, doesn't it?"

I nod and blink, and when I open my eyes he shakes a flask out in front of me.

"Drink all of this. It will make you forget about your leg. Why are you out here in the dark?"

"We were going to sit out here until Brett was in less pain. Then I was going to walk him home."

"Come into the living room. Carsten, in the morning, I'll make you and Brett breakfast with deer sausage. Deer that I killed. Omelets with turkey eggs, and pancakes."

"He hunts," Brett says.

"And watches wrestling apparently."

"I do."

"Did Brett tell you I taught him how to fight?"

"No, he didn't."

The light switch clicks. Strangely, his uncle looks younger from in the picture on the cabinet, even with his facial hair. His face, flushed red, could be placed on Brett's shoulders. Except for his skin color and blond body hair, their bodies are the same. He slides the flask from my hand, drops it in my back pocket, and wraps his arm around my shoulder. Then, he gestures, place your arm in his pit, to Brett.

As we walk sideways into the house, Brett whispers in my ear, "every night should be like this."

And I remind him every night is like this for me.

Chapter 21

Six, five, four, three, two, *zap*, the timer rings, a sound similar to barber clippers but more shrill. Twisting the dial to ten seconds, I then press the PRINT button. A stream of light exposes the negative to paper, and as the cycle ends, the timer clicks and turns the lamp off. Soon after, a young bride and groom appear smiling under a shower of rice. Red rosary beads swing on the machine from the fan's breeze. Pulling from the crucifix to the last circle shrinks how insignificant I feel, after an argument with Father. Penciled notes wallpaper the space beside the enlarger. Rows of destroyed film are pinned above the notes. They remind me that a photographer does not take a photograph. A photographer makes a photograph. Under the red lights, I read his words to my ten-year-old self — 4P's and Double D's.

I whisper, "Double D's," to myself, and I swear I hear him whisper it too, and then he says it louder.

Wiping the sweat from under my nose, I flinch smelling ammonia, vinegar, and rotting wood. A metallic odor spreads through the room. Without the fan, our lungs would burn. Darkroom work is for the obsessed. The darkroom is our mistress that we betray with our wife, the camera. Dust covers a color enlarger from the 70's. Each color has a round knob, cyan, magenta, and yellow, and there are knobs for filter densities. On the floor, beside it, a box sits overflowing with enlarging easels and bulbs for cameras and equipment. Some date back to the 60's and 70's and belonged to grandfather. When father is not in the studio, I take them out of the box one-by-one and line them up on the floor, imagining what they have seen in other rooms with my father and grandfather. Grandfather's judgment looms over us in the form of his all-knowing self-portrait above our heads. In his eyes, everything must be perfect, and so it is. There is not a place where his hand is not present, but it is felt the most in the darkroom. To be before his face, is to be in his presence and feel his mastery and feel smaller, but to also know that my father is a child too.

In a tone reversed for friends, Father speaks to me, but not in a language I comprehend. Foreign word, foreign word, more foreign words, and Cecilia, I heard.

"Say that again."

"You haven't talked about Cecilia in a while."

"Because we have work to do."

"I know that."

"And, it is a distraction."

"Not for me. You can still mention her."

"We have been busy."

"You haven't talked about visiting her either. If it's because of money, I can give you money to take the bus to Chicago."

"Thank you."

"Tonight, see how much a ticket costs."

"Okay, I will."

"Are you afraid of marriage?"

"What time is it?"

"11:45. Why?"

"We have the Khalids at 1:30. I should double check the equipment. I think I forgot to add extra batteries to the pack."

"No, leave it. Tell me and be honest. Are you afraid of marriage?"

"No."

"Are you afraid of girls?"

"No, that's." I stop myself from letting out 'pid, but stu slips. "Strange. A strange thing to say." The way he stressed the word afraid made it sound like he meant something more, something deeper.

"You hate girls?"

"What?"

"Do you hate girls? Are they intimidating? Do you see yourself getting married to Cecilia? Good. I want to see you married before I die."

"You are not going to die."

"When you get married, everyone will be so proud of you."

The wish every African boy makes, in the magical well of imagination, is for his father to be proud of him. When kneeling with clasped hands, this is their prayer, which will guide their life in maturity, in work, in fatherhood, in old age. Sometimes I think if we only spoke about our work, he would show me off, in wallet-size, at dad events like barbecue cook-offs. Somalis believe a child becomes fatherless, without their father's approval, and wanders aimlessly through the world. Often when we are not huddled over trays or cradling cameras, I feel lost in my own center.

Water drips from the print as I attach the drying clip. Father's photographs from the wedding and the ones I shot are as comparable as the colors pink and blue. This photograph is his. The others that are drying are mine. One – the flower girl with thick stockings hides under a tulle mermaid bottom. Two – three women, decades apart in age, in a one-arm embrace, stare critically at something seen off-camera. Three – a woman with bold lipstick and white gloves laughs against a dark background. Maleness is missing from my photographs. Behind me, something splashes, the table shakes, and I hear the rattling of pills, then fan blades. The prescription bottle in his pocket hit the leg. A side cabinet in the front hides the rest of his medications: pain killers, blood thinners, aspirin, steroids, vitamins with foreign names, along with saline spray, ointment, petroleum jelly, Band-Aids, cotton balls, and tissue. A sticker of an eight-fingered hand is on the outside of the cabinet.

"Do you miss her?"

"Who?"

"Cecilia."

"Yes," I say because I cannot tell him, curse word curse word no.

"A ticket back home shouldn't cost more than sixty dollars. I'll give you sixty plus another sixty for next weekend."

"Who will help you shoot and develop?"

"You can stay with your cousin. I'll call him when we get home."

"No. Let me call the bus station first to get prices."

"As soon as you know, tell me. Whatever it is, I will pay it. We need to speed this up."

"Were you afraid of getting married?"

"Yes. I knew so much then, but I didn't want to give up photography. She wanted me to."

"I'm sure she didn't know."

"She did know," he loud talks over me.

"What did marriage teach you?" I ask facing the bride and groom.

After a long uncomfortable pause, he says, "If you can't resolve your problems in peace, you can't solve them in war."

Even without seeing his face, I know he smiled saying it, and I know he swallowed three pills, instead of one. Overwhelmed with this knowledge, I look for familiarity and find it in the film, the notes, the beads, and grandfather. One day I will look up, and I won't see these things.

Chapter 22

Plastic pushes photo paper and a high heel floats to the top. The letters P. L. E. A. S. E. appear on one line, followed by the words, *use another bathroom*, on another line, in a sign above the flower girl's head. Black marker turned precious under the flash. In a rush to use the bathroom, she hurls the bouquet at the sign, with one leg kicked up high. The tightly pinned peach roses burst into petals, stems, and lace. This picture ends my story of the young bride and groom's wedding. We have about twenty prints to develop, before finishing. The word, please, written in black marker, shimmers like the contours of Brett's knife. The word, please, is never heard from the lips of Somali men. Since, it is not an entry word in the Somali dictionary. Therefore, I should have known disappointment would greet me soon after Father said, *please drive to the museum* last year. After winning a grant from the county, we signed up for a class at the Museum of Contemporary Photography. Having worked as a photographer for over thirty years, our instructor was also an attorney. A black and white image that he shot and showed us kindled a fiery discussion. The center of interest was a blond crying holding up a poster that said, less than isn't equal. Piercing and strong, best describe his stare past the camera. The background was an empty courtroom and beside him the ghostly figure of a man edited into the photo. The man's partner (the word the instructor used) was struck crossing the street by a driver on a hit and run rampage. Six people died under the front end; however, the husband suffered only a broken leg.

I tried to hold onto every detail in the story. Somewhere in the middle, my thoughts whirled away and drifted to Manhattan to Seventh Avenue to the driver. I pictured myself bundled up in his seat on Valentine's Day and wondered how it felt watching the life drain out of a man. Through the cracked windshield, Father's eyes stared back at me, and I punched the gas pedal. My ink pen clacked, hitting the floor. After a simple surgery on the fifteenth, the husband died from blood clots in his lungs.

"The widower filed a wrongful death suit against the hospital. The appellate court concluded he didn't have the right to sue because he and his partner were men," the instructor said.

My hand moved to raise a question, but seeing Father's fist stopped it from rising above my ribs. Father stared over his shoulder multiple times at the cat-shaped clock and huffed. Someone behind me started huffing seconds after him. The instructor ignored them. There was a lesson to the story that would prepare us to become greater artists. And it was – photojournalism is about finding the story's best image as a way to render text detachable. To explain, he pointed out parts of the photo I had not noticed: an enhanced wedding ring around the ghost's hand, a smoking gavel, and missing courtroom seats.

"New York law allows not only spouses to sue for wrongful death, but also parents, children, siblings, grandparents, uncles, aunts, and cousins," the instructor continued telling us.

Father's fountain pen popped against the table, and I nervously glanced over at him. He scooted – cursing under his breath – to the edge of his seat and looked like he was preparing to stab the instructor in the eye. I feared for the instructor's life. Father was capable of anything. He huffed and right on cue the person behind me huffed too.

"The couple met on Long Island in 1985," the instructor continued. "Eleven years later they were joined in a civil union and."

He stopped speaking mid-sentence and I looked to where his eyes were at the baby-faced college student. Tears were coming down his cheeks. In a soft voice, he said he planned to marry his boyfriend, and could not imagine slamming against that concrete wall of grief.

"Khaniis," Father whispered.

Then, the Latina sitting behind me whispered a derogatory Spanish word.

I wanted to stand up and yell, curse word you, at both of them. I could not of course, or flying fists would have cracked open my chest.

"Or do you not know that the unrighteous will not inherit the kingdom of God?" Father said, quoting from the Bible. "Do not be deceived; neither fornicators, nor idolaters, nor adulterers, nor the effeminate, nor homosexuals, nor thieves, nor the covetous, nor drunkards, nor revilers, nor swindlers, will inherit the kingdom of God."

The student said, "No it is actually. Know ye not that the unrighteous shall not inherit the kingdom of God? Be not deceived: neither fornicators, nor idolaters, nor adulterers, nor the effeminate called malakoi, nor abusers of themselves with mankind called arsenokoites. Nor thieves, nor covetous, nor drunkards, nor revilers, nor extortioners, shall inherit the kingdom of God."

I wrote the word malakoi in my notebook as tiny as possible to prevent Father from noticing the letters from his seat. The Encyclopedia Britannica at the library in downtown Chicago did not have an entry for it, when I snuck there five days later. However, the male librarian that always winked at me helped me research the word. Originally from Wisconsin, he always told me how he liked to drink beer while eating pancakes, and he had the slight belly and the larger behind to prove it.

"God's same words," Father said, in response to the student.

"It's man's word," the student shouted. "Malakoi means spiritually weak. When Paul wrote Corinthians, it didn't mean homosexual. He was talking about boys who had anal sex with older men for money."

"Gross! Please, stop," the Latina said.

Father stared at her with such love that I expected a proposal. I assumed she was a lesbian and regretted laughing with her before class. I even offered her a peppermint.

The student continued, "The sin is prostitution not attraction. A translator made it effeminate. Arsenokoites doesn't easily translate into English. It referred to an outlawed sexual act between men and women and men and men at that time. A translator made it homosexual. They aren't about loving relationships between two men."

"Loving relationships do not exist between two men," Father said.

"Everyone I wanted to say," the instructor said.

The student yelled, "That was the King James version written in 1611. The John Wycliffe version, written in 1380, is whether ye know not that wicked men shall not wield the kingdom of God. Do not ye err, neither lechers. A lecher is a man addicted to sex, which became fornicator. Neither men that serve false gods, neither adulterers, neither lechers against kind, neither they that do lechery with men, neither thieves, neither avaricious men, covetous men or niggards, neither men full of drunkenness, neither cursers, neither raveners shall wield the kingdom of God. The sin is."

"Sin. You are stupid," Father said.

"I studied the Bible. I didn't learn to single out a group of people."

Watching the student debate with my Father, I became aroused at his comfortability with himself, and around strangers. I photographed his face with my eyes, focusing on the frozen youthfulness; the plastic pink lips; the scratch mark beside his mouth, the pinched nose, almost elfish. He was carefully groomed – maybe even wearing makeup – and not quite a man, but long beyond being a boy. I photographed the name written on his shirt pocket while trying to remember what his last name was to find him in the phonebook. However, I could not put a finger on the name he said.

My Father stood up, scowling the student until the student snatched his schoolbag and stormed out.

Everything in my body welled up as if inflamed. I wanted to grab my chair and beat my father until he could not hurt anyone else. When we returned to the studio, I tampered with development solution, destroying negatives of pictures we shot during a bikini competition. A men's magazine hired us to shoot the women. Father lost three hundred dollars on that assignment. As did I, but I gained something greater – dignity. The women now live on the wall in front of him. That was one of the four times that I saw Father cry. To a photographer, a destroyed negative is worse than death because the negative is lost forever. However, the memory of death sleeps and wakes with everyone who experiences it.

Chapter 23

A photograph of a man's knife-slashed stomach floats in a black frame beside my dresser. His scar goes from his left hairy nipple, zigzags and goes up and around his chest and under his armpit. Little nicks along the zigzag resemble fern fronds. A rounded chunk of flesh is missing on the lower right side. Thin, finger-long welts dent his pasty belly. The man is holding his turtleneck sweater up, and the camera angle decapitates him. Brett traces his finger across the white man's scar. His work shirt rises, exposing the waistband of his pink underwear. The fear and desire that I am experiencing is so palpable that I might collapse and die this morning. Father could catch Brett in my room, and Brett and I could end up carved up like the man in the picture. Instead of a stark white background, a silver exam table would be behind us. Fortunately, the job that Father left for ten minutes ago is an elaborate wedding fifteen miles away.

"All these photos on the wall," Brett says. "And you have more photos of women than men. That's strange considering," Brett says and laughs.

"Considering men are more photogenic than women."

"Exactly."

"Then let me take your photo."

"Let me use the bathroom first," Brett says and walks on an invisible tightrope, one foot ahead of the other, into my open bathroom.

The photography editor at The Tribune told me my work questions past and present events. He saw this through tight close-up shots of female Somalis, Ethiopians, Russians, Germans, and Puerto Ricans. Portraits are sensual and intimate; a relationship builds between the photographer and the sitter. I hold my camera close enough to welcome in the sitter's warmth. That intimacy in a session, I try to avoid, one-on-one with men, especially attractive men. However, many of the male portraits that I have shot, I have them hidden. Next to the dresser, on the floor, is a trunk with a brass decorative handle that Father gave me. It belonged to grandfather. Photographs of mine that are not publishable as determined by my father, and, therefore, have no place in a portfolio I store in the trunk. Some of the hidden photos lie buried at the bottom of the trunk. Seven portfolios, full of my photography, are stacked behind the shaving box. As a photographer, I am interested in mastery of technique through filters, lens, lighting, equipment and environment. Each portfolio represents a different stage in my development.

In two minutes, I have my portable backdrop assembled in front of the wall where Marian is singing. I unravel the white paper background to hide the wall. The black-framed pictures and posters would shift attention away from Brett, with their own narratives. I hold the jagged end of the paper down with seven oversize books. The bathroom doorknob clicks as I move the tripod in front of the background.

"What's that red stuff in the sink?" Brett asks.

"Clay from a mask. I washed my face earlier."

"What's all this?"

"I want to do something like Avedon. Plain white background. Black and white film."

"Make me look important," Brett says.

The contrast of his pink underwear against my blue walls would make a provocative photo on masculinity and desire. I have never seen a man wear masculinity and femininity the way he does as if it is a lace scarf, its unthought, part of his uniform. This blending of gender is a flirtatious performance that I love watching. His masculinity is not enclosed in aggression, and his femininity is not centered on his love of pink, but his sensitivity, gentleness, and strength. Since yesterday, his beard has grown in thicker, and his curly hair is spiraled with tighter curls.

I laugh watching him standing still, not sure what to do, maybe nervous. It is the equivalent of entering a room with an almost domesticated jackal captured in the wild, not dangerous anymore yet dangerous still. Watching him through the viewfinder, he walks to the tripod, grabs the camera, and flips it around.

"Smile."

The high-powered flash turns the room white. The room is white, then red, and then a million colors.

"You can add your picture now," he says.

Grinning like a schoolboy, he scoops his hand around the curve of my back. His lips, an opening redness, brush my bottom lip. His kiss is the equivalent to peeling mangoes with a knife: a knife for meat, danger for pleasure, and a burst of juice on the tongue, then down the throat. When this sweetness collected in the bowl of my imagination, it would turn rancid prematurely. I would leave it on the kitchen countertop of my mind untouched until I was curious again. Now knowing it, this pleasure, that bitterness seems wasteful. Eventually, Brett and I are out of our underwear on my bed with our tongues in each other's mouth. We are black and tan cutouts against white sheets. Our bodies become tangled and twisted up like a salted pretzel, unrecognizable from its previous body.

The one room in our house without photography equipment is my bathroom, the reason I spend no more than ten minutes in here. Even when using skin care products, I slather them on and continue working, in my bedroom, to feel anchored. But for half an hour I have been crying over the sink, with the water running. After Brett and I laid down from exhaustion and dozed off, I woke up with his arm draped over my chest. The heaviness of it terrified me. Men, who love the person they are sleeping next to, hold them in that way. Love, lover, boyfriend, Brett, the words rolled around in my mouth and solidified on my tongue, becoming real. They were as real as the photographs hanging on the walls. Under the shadow and weight of Brett, the tears started. What I experienced was a miracle of mirrors and transformation and looking at myself through an unexpected lens – the other side of the camera.

"What are you doing in there?" he asks, with his mouth close to the door.

"Washing my face."

"Please open the door."

The hinges crackle. Through the small crack, first I see Brett's pubic hair, then his lean body when the door is fully open. Naked and boyish, Brett erases his erection with cupped hands in between his legs. Remove all forms of femininity from Brett, clothing and mannerisms, and he is still himself, but bare and perfect. In my head, I am photographing him. One day, I will shoot him the way he is now, a silhouette, and move him in exaggerated poses to feminize the shape of his body.

"I heard something downstairs," he says.

His head turns toward the door inviting me to listen. In his profile, I see a teenager becoming a man; a magnetism that could go unnoticed if there were more explicit details. That transformation is an aspect of men that is quieter and more narrative, I think, in part because men rarely see it themselves.

After staring at the bedroom door for four minutes, Brett asks, "Are you cool?"

"What did you hear?"

"I don't hear it anymore."

"Do you hear things no one else does?"

"You know what."

"What?"

"I like you," Brett says and kisses me before I can respond.

His words permeate my room in the same way perfumes spread from wall to wall in an unventilated room, and suddenly I smell frankincense, earth, and dampness.

His body is warm; mine is pliant, moving with him. He kicks something on the floor. Book pages rustle. Avedon's *Portraits* opens to Dorothy Parker's basset-hound eyes exposing Brett's knife. We lie down in bed, surrounded by pictures of my father and brothers and working men I have known all my life. The space between our bodies smells like underarm must and mint mouthwash. I grab his hand, stare at the dedication and lines, and kiss it. I love the male body, but in particular I love hands. They carry answers as equally as the face and, like the face, can express every emotion. A hand slams a car door somewhere far away on Evergreen.

Brett's finger pokes my chest with the emotional tone of an exclamation mark. "Have you told your dad you're not going to marry your ex-girlfriend?"

"No."

"What are you scared of?"

"That he'll kill me."

"What you think will happen, already has. You don't know how he'll react until you tell him."

As Brett says the word he'll, in my head, I see the word hell. Hell and he'll sit on the front of my brain and poke and poke and poke. I get a slight headache staring up at the dotted globs of white paint on the ceiling. In Chicago, I would stare up at the ceiling in my room asking myself how could I be manlier. In Father's eyes, I wasn't man enough. His love teetered over my manliness, or lack of it and his love changed, becoming greater than, when I started dating my girlfriend. The day I ended the relationship with my girlfriend and was faced with telling him, I thought about jumping off our apartment building. I talked myself up to the roof, but when I looked out into the world, I saw the pictures I would never take. I pulled myself from the edge and decided not to tell Father about my girlfriend or the roof.

A thumping sound similar to bags dropping on the floor downstairs shocks me and my head bangs against Brett's head.

"Carsten," Father yells from downstairs.

"Shit," Brett says and jumps out of bed.

Tap, tap, hard-bottomed church shoes step up the stairs.

"Where's my underwear?" he whispers in a panic.

"There," I say, pointing by the dresser and snatch my boxer briefs off the floor. Behind me, I hear a noise I should not hear, a quick click and creaking. I thought I locked the door. My father is coming into the room. Brett is naked bending over. I am naked and frightened, with my only form of protection being the underwear I'm holding. Often my thoughts are in Somali and I translate them before speaking. Dhimo, I see the word before I say to myself, "we are going to die."

"Carsten," Father yells from behind the door.

Both my hands drop to cover my genitals with the balled up boxer briefs. I hear a soft sliding sound behind me, and something bumps my bare foot. At my feet, I see the knife that Brett gave me. I grab it quickly.

Father's head moves up, to the side, and back in surprise. "Where are your clothes?"

"I was about to shower."

"Well, don't. Get dressed and come downstairs. Cecilia's waiting for you."

"What? Why is she here?"

"You are getting married, and you haven't —"

"We aren't getting married."

"Yes, you are. Stop talking. Come downstairs now," Father says and exits, making his decision final.

I fly to the door, fast, like an Ethiopian White-backed Vulture on a rotted bushpig, pushing the door closed. Father's church shoes crunch on the wood flooring at the bottom of the stairs. The thin door lock, cold at the touch, makes the tiniest sound, similar to a hiccup from a mouse. Everything in my body gives.

"So you are getting married," Brett says, unseen, from beside my bed, on the floor.

The way his body is, half hidden under the bed, and with his face tense he is aged ten years.

"I'm seventeen. I'm not getting married. My father's insane."

Reassured, Brett's body collapses onto the floor like a failed soufflé. He drags his left leg out from under the bed. Had he moved more under the bed, he would have knocked over a pile of books. Then, Father would have found the boy he banned me from seeing, hiding in my room with an erection. The knife thuds, hitting the floor. I had stuffed it inside my underwear.

"What was that?"

"The knife."

"Would you have used it on your father?"

"I don't know."

Brett's fists press against his wrinkled forehead. A pink sticky note floats to the beige carpet, unstuck from the bottom of his arm. I wrote out a list of equipment to bring to a wedding on the note.

"Cecilia is downstairs. What am I going to do?"

"Go downstairs and tell your father you're not going to marry her."

For a second, I try to see it. What I see is a gray world flipped upside down, a reverse snow globe. The snow is ash. Imagining telling my father I like men, I feel as if I am falling forward fast off the bed, face-first to the floor, even though I'm not falling.

"Relationships aren't photographs," Brett says. "You can't edit out parts you don't like. That's called lying."

I stare at the knife and the underwear in my hand, unsure what to do. Three minutes pass.

"You should go down now. Take my watch and your knife. Put them in your pocket to help you."

As I walk downstairs, the quiet that follows makes me think of the 'L' train in Chicago and the metal on metal roar of old trains hurtling past an old city. The quiet concerns me more than my safety. At all the train stations in downtown Chicago, it is always quiet before the roaring.

Chapter 24

Pushed from behind by distraction, my foot kicks a tin box on the floor. The lid pops open. The mirrored top and metals glint. Buried under grandfather's cufflinks, mother's wedding band, a wedding cord, a red seed bracelet, a Bobby pin, a Cuban coin, and a tooth, there is a gold thorn necklace. Most of the gold flaked off inside the tin. I bought it for Cecilia from Ford City Mall to wear to prom. Tenth-grade year, when I asked her to be my girlfriend, I was not asking her out, I was asking my father to not see me as weak. Womanhood would have pumped oxygen into the lungs of our new relationship. Every time I kissed her was a chance to be the son he wanted. However, every time I kissed her confirmed I was not another Junior.

I can taste her lip gloss now – cherry vanilla.

In January of tenth-grade, I received permission from the school to work off campus at The Tribune. The time that Cecilia and I hung out shriveled up from every day to once a week. Sometimes less. Her absence was nourishment. And, I could taste its sugary sweet juice. It was as if God had kissed my head and given me an excuse to breathe and dream behind cameras. The editor of the school newspaper cornered me downtown months later, shaking me awake. Cecilia confessed to his girlfriend that she wanted to have sex after prom. We had performed every sexual act that I wanted to have with a girl except vaginal, oral, or anal. I would force myself to finger her, and then scald my hand, washing it with soap, shampoo, alcohol, and dishwasher detergent. Her vagina smelled like cold beer and warm puppy breath. When she wanted to go further, I hung religion over her head like a crown of ash crosses. Eventually, I stopped clipping my fingernails.

On accident, a fingernail flicks a frame on the wall as I listen for her voice. Father's dominates the conversation in the dining room.

The day of prom, Father left a condom on my desk, with a note that said, "Proud of you, son." I kissed the word and said it out loud, repeating it as if it were a prayer. He stacked peppermints around the condom in a circle. I waved my hand back and forth under the light cast from the gold wrapper. Neither of us mentioned it when he adjusted my cummerbund that night. The foil crinkled each time Cecilia's thighs rubbed from my thighs to my crotch on the dance floor. One of the edges folded back and scratched my leg through the pocket lining.

Dwelling on that detail, I rub the spot where there used to be a jagged scar. Fingers snap in the dining room.

At midnight, our school principal kicked everyone out of the Crystal Garden at the Navy Pier. Cecilia's girlfriend invited us to a party at the Four Seasons above the Nine Hundred Shops on Michigan Avenue. I hoped the party would weaken her to yawns so I could drop her off by her curfew at two in the morning. The room lights were off, and the drapes pulled back. Body odor, cologne, girlhood, alcohol, and anticipation weighed down the hot air. I saw the outlines of more bodies than I expected. My girlfriend squeezed my hand, leading us around high heels, church shoes, plastic cups, crushed flowers, and over things that crunched under my feet. I bumped into a table. Thick liquor bottles clinked. I grabbed the edge, and a rose prickle pricked my finger. A voice moaned, mimicking my pain but sexualizing it. Smacking, gulps, sucking, zippers unzipping, and candy wrappers unwrapping were like a compass guiding us either in the direction of kissing, drinking, undressing or freshening our breath. Cecilia poured our drinks, heavy, thankfully. In the dark, I bent over and rammed my fingers down my throat, vomiting up the chicken, sweet potatoes, broccoli, and salad that I ate. While the people beside us rushed to the other side of the room, my girlfriend grabbed my hand and hurried into the bathroom. She wiped splatter off of my tuxedo and then cleaned up the vomit in the room. We left to a thunderous applause.

Father's voice stomps the thunder out into an uncomfortable silence. The word *love* falls from his mouth, and I stumble on the stairs. Attraction is not a flashlight switch that can be clicked off. In the past, I wished I could blind myself from seeing the beauty in men, to be an ordinary black flashlight on a white perforated shelf in a discount store and be like my Father. But, at this moment, I don't.

With my head stretched away from hers, I assumed the stench on my breath would squash Cecilia's desire to have sex. My hand cupped the hardness in my pants. She wanted it in the car, parked where we were, on a side street two blocks from the hotel. We looked like a newlywed couple – Cecilia in a white dress and me in a white tuxedo jacket with balloons smothering us in the back seat. I pretended I was too nauseous to push my tongue into her mouth. She drove Junior's car, heelless and in silence, back to my house. Then, she waited for the city bus outside in the cold. I watched her from my bedroom window smoothing the wrinkles out of her wedding dress. The bus arrived, and she waved without moving her hand from the front seat. I felt sorry for the both of us.

The condom had fallen from my pocket onto the bed. I walked into the bathroom, dropped the wrapper in the sink, and lit it on fire with a matchstick. I unpinned the rose boutonniere and dropped it into the fire, then urinated on them.

As I pass by her photograph, on the last step of the stairs, I try to pick out soft plump lies to tell Cecilia. Once found, they escape my mouth in a boyish rush and feel too formal. New words that follow me to the corner seem brutal. When people speak with brutal honesty, the brutality, not the honesty is remembered the most. The bottom of a chair scrapes the carpet as someone stands up in the dining room, and I dig the bottom of my feet into the floor. I want to turn away, to run out the front door, but if run, I won't be moving the way my blood beats. Thorns from a bush planted by a shaken man prick deeper than other thorns. The scratches and the ugliness ahead give me the chance to be the son I need to be – prepared to fight.

Chapter 25

Legs wobbly, but determined to speak, I lean back, listening to their voices.

"Carsten," Father yells from the opposite side of the wall.

An electric shock jolts my hand. The sensation stings, spreading up to my shoulder, then onto my skin. A patch of bumps burst out on my wrist. The bumps itch; I scratch and loose balance. My hand crunches as it lands flat on the console table. The smell of citrus and mint rises up from the bundle of khat. The leaves snap as I pluck them off the stalk. I roll a wad of leaves into a little ball and pack it down inside my right cheek – the way Father showed me. The taste is green, sour, and unpleasant. Six bundles are wrapped in banana leaves, tied with string, and twisted at the bottom. Evergreen glistens under lime. I chew more leaves and stuff the lump beside the little ball, squashing my tongue against the mass. Slime dribbles down the edge of my mouth. Meat, men's cologne, mint, and fresh cut grass bounce on the surface of the summer air. I should smell kiwi and melon from Cecilia's signature perfume. I hear two clicks, possibly from a cigarette lighter. The scents thin out and frankincense carpets the hallway. In the dining room, Ricky's voice squeaks and Junior whispers. Our Father, who doesn't art in heaven, is giddy, attaboy-patting Ricky for kissing a girl. I shiver and slump against the wall. The bronze rooster vibrates on the table. My hand swings, rubbing the knife in my pocket. To hide the bulge, I hold my hand over my thigh. In my other hand, I squeeze Brett's watch and then shove it in my pocket. I rub the rooster's pearl bone, before rushing through the doorway to madness.

Father and Ricky sit, laughing at the table, taking up more space than necessary. Clean-shaven, but curse-filled, Father looks fifteen pounds heavier. He stabs the air with a child-like excitement that would've forced me to smile on a different day. Slouching against the same wall I had been eavesdropping behind, Junior calls me over, but I ignore the gesture. I search for clues a woman would leave – a lip smudge, a folded napkin, a purse, or perfume. Pizza boxes, chicken wings, garlic bread, string beans, two cakes, khat leaves, tea mugs, plates, and a soapstone pot hide the tabletop. The fourth plate is the only plate missing food. Glancing back, I notice medical tape binds Junior's index and middle finger together on his right hand. His left fist is under his right triceps. The telephone sits propped in the crook of his neck. The puffiness under his eyes, his receding hairline on the sides, the roundness of his belly, and his hairiness betray his youth.

"No, I'm not dating her," he says into the telephone. "We met yesterday in downtown."

"Where's Cecilia?"

"On the phone with Junior," Father says.

"He's out now. I'll put him on," Junior says.

The triangular space where my chest and stomach meet becomes wet as Cecilia says, "goodbye." A cemetery quiet falls. From behind the wall, I hear the soft suction sound of a door closing. I slide the knife from my pocket and hide it between my thighs on the seat.

With an expression appropriate for church, Father asks, "What did she say?"

"You said she was here."

"She was here. On the phone. Luckily, Junior talked to her, so she did not realize it took you thirty minutes to come downstairs. Did she tell you she is coming to visit?"

"I have something to tell you."

"She's pregnant. Isn't she?" Father says. "I knew it."

"No."

"You're seeing someone else and she is pregnant."

"Let him talk," Junior says.

"I like men, not girls."

Father shapes his mouth into an O, opening wide, imitating Marian Anderson in the Richard Avedon poster. Where she becomes a beautiful creature, he becomes a grotesque giant capable of tearing a child to shreds with a swat of his claw. With murder in his eyes, he throws his mug across the table. The chipped handle cuts my shoulder before shattering to the floor.

"No, you are not khaniis." Saying the word khaniis, he turns his face up as if he smells fresh shit. "You are not like that. Tell me that. Say it."

"I like men."

His pounding fist rattles the table. The incense burner tips over, spilling charcoal and ash. Two cowry shells break off. As I hop up to run, Father yanks my chair from under the table. The knife drops. Now, all that I have left is my voice. He punches me in the side. The pain flips the room over on its head. I blink twice and realize I'm staring up at the ceiling. He straddles me, locking my arms in place. A glob of spit slips down my cheek to my neck. He smears his mucus and salt into my face as if cleansing me of my mortal sin. I clench down on my teeth to prepare for his knuckles. My mouth bleeds from the second and third punches. On the fourth blow, my nose bleeds. The next hit catches me in the ribs as I take a breath. I squeeze my fists, pushing the pain inward, to not scream.

"I will beat it out of you."

"You asshole," Junior yells and punches him in the face.

Father flops to the floor and crawls to the china cabinet. From beside it, he hurls the herder's headrest at Junior, striking him in the front of his leg. Hearing a whump sound against bone, I flinch in pain. Ricky runs, wailing, out of the room. A door slams, seconds later.

"What's wrong with you?" Junior yells.

"I told that woman not to eat so much sugar when she had you. She was addicted to pies, cakes, and cookies. That is how babies become sweet."

"That's stupid," Junior says.

"Khaniis burn in hell."

"Why even say that nonsense?" Junior says.

"I am not talking to you."

"What's so wrong with liking men?" Junior says.

"I will kill you after I kill him first."

He charges straight. Junior slaps away his fist. His

body transforms into a shield, with his hands stretching out to the side. I step where he steps, two steps to the left.

"Think about what is going to happen to you. You're going to die alone."

"Like you," Junior says. "The only person that loves you is Carsten. If you push him away, you'll be alone. I'll leave you the first chance I get."

He pulls his head back to the right, slipping away from a punch. Furious and focusing his spite, Father stabs him in the chest with his finger, then points at me.

"Why would you want to live like a nasty animal?"

"Why can't you accept this?" Junior says.

"I'm still your son."

"You are not my son anymore. I have two sons."

Everything that I could say to Father, I swallow leaving him and Junior to wallow in the heaviness of hatred, misery, and love.

"Don't you dare. Only a woman would walk out this way," Father yells.

I suck my teeth without thinking about it.

"Suck your teeth like a little girl."

My faith in our Father dissolves down my body, into my feet, into the floor, freeing me.

"Fuck you. Go to hell."

"Don't talk to me like that," Father says.

"But you can say whatever you want."

"That is not a life you want for yourself."

"Yes, it is."

"How do you know?"

"I know."

"Have you had sex with a man?"

My throat tightens hearing the scraping sound as the

nail rips from the wall. I follow the line from the ball of his shoulder to the point of the frame. Junior punches his hand – the photograph falls, smashing, to the ground – then he locks Father's arms behind his back.

"Leave my house right now."

"No. Don't," Junior says.

"Yes. Do. Leave. Dog."

Thrashing as if possessed, he jerks his right arm away, and elbows Junior in the stomach. Junior bends at the knees, hugs himself, and vomits.

Being flung out onto the street was one of my fears. My fear was a flat country of plains and plateaus, red and brown, in the Horn of Africa, shaped like the rhino's horn. I could look at the future in the distance, which was a mirage of never-ending nightmares: prostitutes in Boystown, homeless boys my age, and feminine men with black eyes. Their recommendations were the same – do not say a word.

I try to look Father in the eye from where he is standing at the bottom of the stairs. He shakes his head the way men at Cecilia's church shake their heads, side-to-side, mm-hmming with their lips pressed tight together. Then, he looks away across from the stairs. My eyes follow his, at the framed print hanging up on the wall. The photograph is a glittering fireworks display, in a cloudless night sky, above the clock on State Street. The black Roman numeral dials turn the clock's face milk white. The *Chicago Tribune* printed it on the front-page on January 11, 1980. He shot it with his Diana camera. What I find fascinating about the photograph is how massive the clock appears. As a boy, I wanted to wake up and live in that dream world where magical fireworks crackle every night before bed.

The back of Father's church suit that he wore to the wedding reflects on the glass. As his suit disappears out the picture, into the living room, the despair I feel bends into a sadness deeper than I have ever felt. There is no mystery left. Here, I am homeless, parentless, futureless, traveling into the nameless nowhere. I am being betrayed, failed, broken, formed, and packed away, a one-wheeled suitcase pushed in the back of the closet of memory to collect dust. Is there anything worse for a son than being forgotten by his Father?

Chapter 26

The stench of vinegar forces me to see I've bunched the sheet into a rope. If I continue down it could twist into a noose. Tie, slipknot, tighten, suspend, and Father's shame will end. All deaths are equal; they are all hyphenated. According to Islamic law, Junior should be smearing oil across my head in a straight line and wrapping me in white cloth. Then, drive to the mosque. There, an emerald cloth with Allah embroidered in gold should be draped over my body. Fortunately, we aren't standing on a land of limited contrast. Here, Fathers aren't as tall as gods.

The sky outside my window is black as a grave. Dressed for a funeral – but I imagine that – Marian Anderson sings to me. The possessed sound from her lips, I need to stand with, walk to, and move away from, but I can't move from the bed or the blanket. By accident, I touch my ribs through my shirt and feel a thick lump under my skin. As I press on it, the possible becomes dreaming in waking. A hot light, attached to a stand, is the only light on in my room. I wish

I could fold every light and my other equipment in half and pack them in my suitcase, but none of it will fit. That is a different dream.

A thumbtack pings, dropping on the nightstand and rattles rolling down an empty frame. Stacked behind it are ten more. Dust flies up from a portfolio. Down feathers scatter on top of it. Plastic crackles as I flip it open to Father shooting a father shooting his son and grandson. I turn the page to the homeless man huddled under the sculpture in Daley Plaza. While clutching his coat, the bones in his hands stick out like spines on a prickly pear cactus. His faded conductor hat whitens his chalky beard. On the next page, there is a drag queen wearing an aluminum foil skirt. She and a blond in a matching Speedo pageant wave under pink confetti in a parade. Caught from the side, her legs endless and her body is a wire coat hanger. A bearded man dressed as a bedazzled nun holds up a poster that says, Our Sex Is Holy Too. His hands, covered in dark hair, resemble bear paws. These are my photographs Father has never seen. As my knee bumps the frame, I slide out Father's photograph from the portfolio. I frame it and hang it beside Marian. Then, I hang the homeless man, the drag queen, and other men I've photographed on the wall.

Staring at the scuff marks on my suitcase, the frame I'm holding slips, and I sink into the bed. In South Africa, I dragged it against a memorial, which left white marks on the front and side. A lapel ribbon wedged into the back wheel during a trip to London. A barcode sticker, unable to peel off, is by the top handle. A hirsute ticketing agent at the airport in Acapulco placed it there. The handwritten luggage tag, from our last trip to Somalia, is fastened to the handle. On each trip, Father and I shot on assignment and lived out of cheap hotels. Now, I will live out of this suitcase on the street.

As I slap the bed, the vinegar smell explodes. It's photo developer that splashed on my hands yesterday. Vinegar and ammonia are my kiwi and melon. All of the faces staring back at me were born under these baths with these hands, except three. They will be without a father too. Thirty minutes passes and half an hour turns to two. My suitcase is empty; however not knowing where I'll sleep tonight is crippling. I slump deeper into the bed; tears come. My door opens and groans, then closes. Where I expect to find Father, instead I find my older brother. The miniature version of him, Ricky, tiptoes in chewing candy.

Sitting down beside me, Junior asks, "Are you going to stay with Brett?"

"How do you know about Brett?"

"Ricky told me. He's seen you two hanging out."

Ricky lowers his head, hiding his eyes.

"It's okay Ricky. I'm not mad. I don't know where I'm staying."

"What about in the room above the studio? You don't use it for anything."

"You're right."

"You already have a key and I can steal his."

"Thanks and thank you for what you did downstairs."

"Have you seen the payphone by the studio? Anything you need, just call, and I'll help."

"Me too," Ricky says. "I won't tell daddy. I promise."

"Thanks, Ricky."

"You know I don't care about you dating Brett," Junior says. "You're my brother, and I want to know what's going on with you."

"Okay."

"Okay," Junior mimics the way I said it. "That bitch is sleep. Stay and leave in the morning. He won't know."

"You said bitch."

Shoving Ricky's shoulder, Junior says, "Go to bed."

Ricky puffs out his chipmunk cheeks, leaving quietly.

"If you're bold enough to have it, you should be bold enough to use it," Junior says and pulls Brett's knife from his pocket. "Also, if you want, I can hide your porn in my room."

"How do you know about that?"

"Ricky told me."

"Damn nosy kid."

"Is Brett your boyfriend?"

"No. We're just friends."

"Tell your boyfriend he needs my approval before he talks to you again."

I punch my brother in the arm, and we both laugh.

Unlike any other night before, I know tonight Junior and me will stay up and talk for hours as a way to hold onto this crumbling time that we have left. It might never happen again. Friendship is a foreign language our Father failed to teach us. It forced us to translate, and we violated the language.

In the fifth grade, Junior started dating a Puerto Rican with blue eyes and a love of red lipstick. By sixth grade, he was dating a Russian girl. Seventh through tenth, he dated a different girl every month. Family dinner conversations always drifted to Junior and his women. Eventually, he would ask, "When are you getting a girlfriend?" Father waited, often with a glimmer of hope in his eyes, for my answer. Every time it was, *shut up*.

Ninth-grade year, when Junior moved in with Grandfather, I savored the silence. For the first time, I invited my friend over to our apartment. We kissed on the couch while pretending to watch television. A key crunched in the front door, but we didn't hear it. The door swung open as our mouths moved apart. Junior waddled in eating fries out of a paper bag and plopped down in between us. Instead of questioning him, I ignored him hoping he'd leave. A rapper wearing a zebra Speedo popped on the screen. A mountain of women in bikinis jiggled and gyrated around him. The music video was titled, "Pumps and a Bump." The rapper's low-slinging bump, in the front, bounced. It swung and hit his middle stomach muscle. He had to have stuffed something in his Speedo; at least it appeared larger than possible.

A soft *oh* came out of my friend's mouth, and his hand dropped between his thighs.

Junior started singing the chorus to the rap song, and then stopped and said, "Sing, Carsten. It's okay if you change it to the boys with the pumps and a bump."

The smack of the throw pillow, hitting his head, felt wonderful. Though the punch to my chest, from him, did not. My friend's eyes grew wider watching us fight. And we continued until Junior snatched the remote from my hand. He flipped through channels to a press conference. A man stood at a podium inside what appeared to be a crowded theater. The first words out of his mouth were gay men. Junior howled.

He rambled on saying, "Gay men rub feces all over their bodies during sex for sexual gratification. They're not normal."

"You two play in shit?" Junior asked.

Talking to my brother, I laugh, cry, pack, remember, cry more, and then I am pushed out the house by my black-robed Father and erased as his son. The fatherless world cracks open, like a pop can.

In the summer sky, fireworks, gold, green, white, and red explode at a neighbor's house.

Chapter 27

The storage room welcomes me in with the promise of fire to fat. I transform from teenager to grilled meat with the turn of the lock. Although after walking miles in the heat, even this sauna is a relief. I undress down to my underwear and one-by-one remove the contents of my suitcase: cameras, equipment, portfolio, clothing, junk food, a plastic bag, the knife, pushpins, and Marian Anderson. The weight of unpacking my life strips me down further, past blood, bone, marrow, identity. In Father's eyes, he sees birth date, hyphen, death date, above my name on a grave – and there is no coming back. As long as I sleep here, it will break me knowing drywall and plaster separate me from him. The room is empty, except for three metal shelves with a box of rat traps. Four large windows face out onto storefronts on Main Street below. Wetness spreads over my underwear as I struggle opening the windows. Paint flakes dazzle my hands like glitter. Its heaviness makes me feel lightheaded, and I have to sit.

Sunlight gleams off the metal finish on the Land camera that Father shot with during the 70's. From its classic shape, the camera collapses into a rectangle, slightly smaller than a notebook. The metal parts are hot. My arms become a tripod to sharpen the image of the room. The film sheet inside passes through a pair of rollers and the rollers spread chemicals out onto the sheet. Dyes, acid, and developers react, creating the picture. With instant photography, the magic isn't watching the image appear from whiteness. The magic is the ability to manipulate the image. As it's developing, I take a rusty nail from the windowsill. I etch lines in the top of the Polaroid to highlight the emptiness. Then, I pin it in the space between the middle windows. When I look outside, I can look inside as well. I shoot four more pictures of the room, and as I pin them up, I stick dead moths over them. Their bark-like bodies, hairier than I'd imagine, add texture to the Polaroids.

Snap, I hear behind me, followed by squash, then a double dunt. Walking toward the back, I see the blood and guts of a rodent and the mutilated rat caught in a trap. I grab a newspaper off the rack, scoop the guts and trap inside, and throw it all out of the window. A black cat darts over from across the street, pouncing on it, and drags the trap away. Clacking follows.

Through the windows, the hint of meat cooking drifts into the room. The aroma drowns out the stale air smell. My stomach gurgles, but I'm too tired to open up the world. As a family, we quit eating junk food for Lent. However, the day Lent ended, April 12th, I bought five bags of sugary bites. All of the plastic in the bag rustles as I grab the largest item. I unwrap a cream cheese Danish, devour it, and unwrap another, licking my fingers as I finish the second.

An hour later, as I'm eating another Danish, the entry alert device dings. I lower my head to the floor, listening. Shirtless and pantless, I become stone. Tap tap, I hear, from Father's shoes. If I move, the floor will squeak. The door bells chime. Sweat drips down my stomach as I remember I opened the windows. The door dings and the burden of being discovered sinks to my feet into the floor. *Rip*, I hear. Triplicate paper, possibly. *The mechanical whirring of a printer on its deathbed.* Unclear. *Tap tap.* Church shoes. My nose tingles. I sneeze from breathing in dust. My hand slams down, and a staple rips through my skin. With tears in my eyes, I wait, listening, for the glass door to shatter. Instead, the door to the darkroom slams close. I pull the staple out, and my entire body unloosens. Blood surfaces.

Even with drywall and plaster separating us, in my head, I can see him. He ties a black apron around his neck and slips on goggles and gloves. I am in my underwear upstairs. The safelight lamp, with a red bulb, switches on. I imagine the light in the storage room turns red. Father first feeds the film, to be printed, onto the Paterson reel. He places the reel in the handheld tank, allowing the film to soak in Kodak HC 110. He flips the tank over several times for ten seconds. For thirty seconds, he lets the film rest, and then flips it over for five seconds, stops for thirty seconds, and repeats the last two steps five times. The storage room transforms into a darkroom and in the darkroom, I am standing beside him, watching everything. He pours the developer out of the tank using a funnel. Then, he holds the film under cold water, at sixty-five degrees, for half an hour. The chemical residue, splotches, and fingerprints wash away. And, finally he hangs the film in a drying tank. The process changes the film into negatives.

dropped sounds and running to prepare myself. Minutes go by and nothing. Father continues working. I reach for the jug and set it closer to my face. The yolk-colored liquid resembles Stop Bath. Photographers use Stop Bath to stop the development of film or paper by either washing off developing chemical or neutralizing it. The chemical bath is dark yellow. In the darkroom, we use emptied milk jugs for Stop Bath, Fixer, and Hypo Clear.

My legs shake as I glance at the yellow. I twist off the jug cap in a hurry, almost spilling the liquid on my feet. Hopefully, Father cannot hear the splash of urine against plastic.

Finished, I drop the container close to the wrappers. Twenty-five cents printed in red ink stands out on the packaging. I fan the wrappers around a store receipt, with the nutrition labels showing. Beads of sweat from my forehead drip as I shoot the summer wreath of waste. The word sugar is in bold on each wrapper. My eyes slide down the labels to the letter T, next to an A, followed by N and K. Somehow while in grammar school, I learned pouring sugar into a gas tank could ruin a car engine. The idea was that the heat would melt the sugar, sending granules into every nook. Four years ago, Junior and I poured sugar into our Father's previous car, in retaliation for beating us for playing with a neighbor's dog. After three weeks of disappointment, Junior forced me to ask my science teacher about the rumor.

"Sugar does not dissolve in gasoline," he said. "What do you do if you want to have an effect? Put water in the tank."

Pouring several cups of water into a car causes the fuel pump to fill the fuel lines with water instead of gas.

"The car would still function, but not as well," he said.

After filling Father's car with water, Junior and I observed: the car shook when idling and jerked when accelerating. He had to push the pedal to the floor to accelerate. When he pressed on the brake, the pads screeched. Watching it all happen was beautiful, but I felt guilty. I promised myself I wouldn't allow Junior to talk me into anything unsafe again.

Before I convince myself not to, I ease into my wet shirt and pants. I tiptoe down the steps, listening for the studio door to open. I hurry to Father's car parked in front and with a smile on my face I pour piss from the container into the tank. Looking around, I see the rat's head on the sidewalk.

Chapter 28

Racing up the stairs, I stumble, catch the rail, and break into laughter. Something within my body has changed. Everywhere, all at once, I'm buzzing. My feet banging against the steps give the buzzing a sound. The knotted muscles in my arms that disable me relax. My arms wave like a piñata in the wind. To ground myself, I slap the rail as I run. Wham, the wood vibrates. I feel invincible. With each wobble of the stairs, I gain a newborn confidence. I know how to hurt him back: through a more cruel form of violence. And, where it'll hurt him the worst, in his mouth.

On the street, I notice a blonde wearing a skirt suit, staring up at me. A question is on her lips. Whatever it is, it doesn't matter. She looks terrified.

I rush into the warmth of the storage room and smash my hand over my mouth, smothering the boom in my laughter. My hand smells like dry earth. I laugh louder looking at the shoe prints on the car from the upstairs window. I count thirty. Stomp marks, dents, exposed metal, power, and hunger displayed for the world. I press harder. Even though I want Father to hear me laughing downstairs, he can't hear me now. Although, seeing his nose scrunched up, would be more exciting than Brett's raised eyebrow and open mouth. I could lie, and tell him I'll marry my ex-girlfriend to spread out in the passenger seat the day his car jerks, possessed with the demon of urine. At that beautiful moment, I could reveal I ruined his payment. And after he rammed my head into the glove compartment, my self-hatred would liquefy and bleed out. I would endure everything he had, punches, elbows, teeth, spit, and insults to show him I'm strong. Then, when his body sunk into his seat, I'd crack him in the chest and listen to his power hiss out.

In my palm, goo drips; blood from a splinter I find. It must've come from the rail. I dig it out with my nails and place it on the windowsill. A thread of blood curls away from the splinter. I close the window, in front of me, and then the rest. When Father's jaw drops seeing the stomp marks, he won't see the open windows and run up here. I hear a chattering noise from the back of the room and stare through the glass. My Father glares back at me. The floor squeaks as I spin around. However, Father isn't standing anywhere in the room. I freeze, listening for footsteps from downstairs. Fifteen seconds. Forty seconds. Five minutes. There's only silence. I turn back to the window, and there he is. Is it possible that a chemical process occurred in my body? My eyes, my nose, my skin color, are his. I hold up my hands, and his hands become my hands. Palm creases and veins rearrange themselves. Moles form on my hand in the same place where they are on his hand. A second thumb appears. My calves tingle. I yank my pants down. Fine black hairs spring up from my knees down to my ankles. Together, we, my father and I, bring a third body into the world. Carsten Reed Tynes is born out of memory and blood, immaculate. Carsten Reed Tynes' specialty is violence: fists and rocks and crosses and sticks. His eyes, our eyes, are bloodshot. Beside my bloodshot eyes, there is a red streak on the window. I step right so that the streak hovers over my face. The high I feel fades watching myself distorted in the glass. There is an irrepressible anger inside my body waiting to turn me into a Tynes man. As pleasurable as it was destroying Father's car, I cannot transform into him, the way he transformed into Grandfather. Grandfather's violence is as talked about in our family's village in Somalia as legendary folktales.

In the window's reflection, behind the third body, is the room. The room, a perfect rectangle, has silences where furniture used to be. Before we dumped it, the room had an identity. They were in the world, and of the world, and now are closer to the materials they had been. Scooping my hand under the collar of my shirt, I pull it over my head and kick off my pants. The chattering continues, then I hear running water. Something flashes in the glass. Through the window, I stare at my face, hands, skin, and body. A heaviness washes over me; it vibrates the room. I'm light-headed. The ground beneath seems to be a window. I lean against the wall.

A blond teenager bites into a croissant sandwich on the street. The white paper bag, tucked under his armpit, reads Havington, in gold lettering. White stuccoed and dangerous, Havington is a froufrou delicatessen on the corner of Main and Beverly Road. For the cost of a croissant, a person living on the street could feast for four days. I wondered where were the homeless when Father and I toured downtown months ago. In Chicago, homeless people are downtown's unofficial ambassadors. Ambassadors buzz around and swoop down on lost tourists to direct them in the appropriate direction, for a donation, of course. Looking at the teenager, I realize being homeless in a moneyed neighborhood is equivalent to laying down a glue trap for mice and lying down in the glue. Hunger is not the scariest part of homelessness; being snatched from the place where a person has rooted himself is. What if kicking Father's car causes him to catch me tonight? As I ask myself that while watching the boy, my stomach growls.

Betray your mistress, I tell myself.

My imagined mentor, Avedon, would work from the start of the day to the fall of the blue hour shooting countless rolls of film, for one dramatic photograph.

"Stopping to eat even a morsel is a distraction," Avedon told *American Photo* magazine in an interview previewing his exhibition at the Metropolitan Museum of Art in 1978. That issue, with his black and white photograph of Sophia Loren on the cover, is one item I wish I could've packed. Avedon continued the interview saying, "I believe that you have to love your work so much that it is all you want to do. I believe you must betray your mistress for your work, you betray your wife for your work. And, she must betray you for her work. I believe work is the one thing in the world that never betrays you. That lasts."

Father demanded that I memorize Avedon's quote until the words became imprinted behind my eye, and I could picture the quote upside down, when I looked at the world behind the viewfinder. He called it training, seeing the real world as upside down and seeing the world in front of my camera as corrected. I like to think that Richard Avedon was speaking through my father.

"Stopping to eat," I would hear Father say on shoots.

Those words are powerful.

"Even a morsel," I say watching the teenager disappear.

My suitcase shows its inner contents: neatly refolded clothing around camera equipment. Inspired, I reach down, grabbing the long focus lens, and firmly screw it into my Nikon's mount. I turn the lens clockwise, and when it stops, I give it an extra twist. Then I open the window in front of me. Anger, fear, and hunger are equally important to a photographer as an understanding of light; they can ignite the creative spark.

With the lens tightened, I point the camera out the window. I repeat Avedon's trance-like words and take deliberate pictures of the street, changing out film rolls until the blue hour turns coal black, and I hear my father scream.

Chapter 29

The distance of Father's car complicates the photograph I want. A traffic light casts its color onto a puddle. The car appears to be bleeding from its injuries. With my lens held out the window, I hope the camera captures what I'm after – evidence. The undeniable proof will enhance the picture in my head. Like how children wake from a dream and make-believe, it will be new again. The taillights vanish down the street, and I'm alone with my delight. I wallow in it, forming it into a physical object, then push it in my hand. I squeeze it and spit on the floor. The fluid sticks to the bottom of my feet.

After half an hour, the feeling flips and forms into heaviness. Junior would punch me in the arm while Brett would kiss me hearing I kicked in the car. Their absence increases the heaviness in my head. My body becomes weighted with stones as I slide down the wall.

Around the room, fingernail-like scratches expose layers of paint. A creamy prime coat covers up yellow paint, gray paint, and white paint. Paint chips dazzle the floor. Light from the double-headed lamppost illuminates where the previous owners positioned the posters. Those sections of the wall are brighter from being untouched by sunlight. The corners of the multicolored paper are stuck in time, between the forties and nineties, by heavy-duty staples and tape. I crumple up my shirt and pull two shirts from my suitcase. Placing the shirts behind my head, I practice how I'll tell Junior and Brett about the car and the pictures. *The urine was golden*, I'll start with and I'll end with *running up the stairs*, but instead of running I'll *walk up* the stairs. Walking sounds gutsier.

In the silence, I listen to myself, then I ask questions of myself. Then, I practice talking to myself out loud to become accustomed to how it feels. The words are masculine and massive, much larger than I anticipated. I know what a person says is the mirror to their soul, so I feminize the words, saying them slower and closer to the truth. The truth will lead me to the light. An innocuous humming from the street peels my back from the wall. Listening with intent, I move the mechanical noise into my body, holding on to it, and an unexplainable sorrow enters my bones. Bones in my back, wrist, and legs crack. Even though the room is spacious, the conditions feel coffin-like, cramped and permanent. In Somalia, there is a saying that sorrow is like azuki beans from the market. Take a bowlful a day, and it will come to a delicious end at last. Slipping down the wall, with my shoulders close to touching the carpet of dust, I close my eyes to eliminate a bowlful and fall back asleep.

Hammering outside jerks me awake. A sound like a baritone dolphin whistle reverberates in between the hand pounding. Brett's watch, on my wrist, reveals the time is three thirty in the morning.

"Carsten, open the door," Father yells.

The other way out of the storage room is through a window. Jumping from the second floor could be fatal. However, if Father is banging, then Junior swiped his key. Splitting the door open is the only way he will wrap his eleven fingers around my throat. Though a locked door has not stopped him before.

"Open it," Father yells.

My legs tingle. I snatch the knife from inside the suitcase in preparation for his heel to kick in the door. The weakest part is its lightweight frame. Wood even speaks its own language. I press the bar on the handle and unlock the serrated blade. Gripping the knife tightly, I ram the blade in the air, practicing the movement, to allow it to become part of my body. Short and fast swats. The knife becomes my camera. Across my eyes, images from the other side of the door form. His hands, his position, his posture, they are separate images and critical to my safety.

"It's your brother," the voice says.

As I peek through the crack, hiding the knife behind my back, Junior yells, "Reed came home cursing like a madman. Finally, you grew some balls."

"It felt great."

"I knew you had it in you. You're just like Reed."

"No, I'm not."

"Yes, you are. You can't let him know you're up here. I brought you a flashlight and my sleeping bag." Then, from under his arm, he snatches a hidden bag of chips and says, "It ain't easy being cheesy."

Smiling, the way our father smiles, he shows the gap between his teeth on the side of his mouth. I never acknowledge the missing tooth, because that might remind him how it came out and why I have it in my pocket. Along with it, in my pocket, I have mother's Bobby pin, her wedding band, and the coin that bookmarked a page in her Bible. The love I felt for my brother, as he shielded me from Father, multiplies and overwhelms me now, and I cry. From age five, I assumed Junior despised me for being the opposite of him. Perhaps aggression was his way of expressing love, but his idea of brotherhood was turned on its head and trapped in a chokehold. Although when we were younger, chokeholds were received as frequently as a late breakfast from our Father. And from our Father, we are floating, but it's the brilliance of the morning sun that reminds us Father is predictable. He arrives at eight in the morning every day to work. We hug and don't look at each other as we say goodbye in Somali. The brave interested in speaking Somali also have to understand poetry. Allusion, proverbs, and rhyme pepper the language. So our goodbye wasn't goodbye; it was a flower wrapped in its bulb, like a root-vegetable and thrust into the light. The light will linger a little longer today. Then, I won't be as lonely.

Standing, hunched over the window, I watch Junior's car vanish in the opposite direction Father drove. Across the street, multiple flyers that create a single dollar sign flap in the wind. Five minutes later, Father's car cries like a donkey begging for sugar beets and parks in front at eight o'clock. Then, under my feet, I hear splat, something hefty thrown in the studio, followed by *fuck*, and I smile.

Chapter 30

The seeing eye Labrador, stuffed under my seat, licks the back of my ankle. Jolted, I swing my foot forward. Blonde hairs are stuck to the vinyl floor. Dried pop has shaped a spider web of sugar. The dog's owner, an elderly blonde, mumbles something that sounds like Russian. Her gold chain necklace has a babushka doll pendant with stripes and swirls of color. The Styrofoam container, in a plastic bag on the seat beside her, reeks of horseradish. Or maybe it's on her breath. All the Russian students in Chicago smelled like horseradish. My sambusa lunches tasted richer with their borscht, lamb shashlik, cabbage pirozhki, or rolled pancakes with fruit jam. My stomach growls. Would she know if I took her bag?

The bus stops at a boarded up building with a mural of an underwater world. The sun, painted lime green and in flames, is the focal point. Multicolored mermaids, bearded mermen, imaginary creatures, and decomposing flowers contrast the sun. The color mixing, shading, and layering creates a photographic image. It looks staged, shot underwater, blown up, and wheat-pasted. I yank the hanging cord gawking at one of the mermen. The stop requested sign glows.

Like Brett, he has soft features but is otherwise unfeminine. The light brown hair and eyebrows and dark eyes look exactly right. In his lips, there is the beginning of a smile. The delicate mouth highlights the prominent nose. Standing behind cameras, pushes photographers to notice eyes, noses, and mouths more than other people. Jewel-toned scales plunge down his fin and spreading tail. The algae-covered rock he sits on accentuates their brilliance. I adjust my camera to prevent overexposure to the picture from the morning sun. Given distance, I realize telling the truth is like taking a picture. Through the lens, the photographer has to find meaning, something necessary to share. Being behind a camera, helped me avoid telling my father I wanted to be with a man. It became easier dealing with what was in my camera lens, than what was in front of me in life. I was afraid. Fear was just as much a part of me as a scar. The shame I covered the scar with was a cocoon, and I became my fear. In my bedroom, I'd stare up at the ceiling, wishing I could remake myself into what a man should be, but what makes a man? Not being female. Having a penis. Testosterone. Thick body hair. Being a copy of the Marlboro Man. Aggression. Presence in a crowded room. An absence of fear. I don't know how to define being a man. However, I do know I want to be a man who isn't afraid to share who he is. There are all kinds of fear. Having to cross out an entire part of your life with a grease pencil, may be the worst kind.

Someone graffitied a French fry carton on a trash bin in front of the building. The carton has a protruding stomach. A miniature fry, drenched in ketchup, is falling from its lips. The fries are knife-shaped. For me, yellow and taste are married. The potatoes in sambusa are saffron. Ripe plantains are brownish-yellow, dappled with black, and ready to fry. Sweet tulumba is the color of burnt sugar. Blended mango juice, with milk, yogurt, and sugar, is more chartreuse than orange. My favorite foods are yellow. Hunger pangs force my feet to follow meat cooking in the opposite direction from the DIA. The scent intensifies. On the sidewalk, yellows become bolder than other colors: the cheese in a window display, the words in junk food wrappers, and the hair on a spray painted bombshell. At the cross street, 6th, a hot dog seller set up an elaborate stand with a dog-shaped counter. The position of the grill places his back to the customers. Four rickety tables with foldable chairs are beside the stand. Two blond businessmen wearing black suits sit at one table eating hot dogs. A blonde sitting facing the street looks as if she is waiting for hers. The seller rolls a bacon-wrapped dog through onions, green peppers, and a chili. A clock-sized sign, with neon dots circling around blackness, reads one hundred percent beef. The seller places a paper food tray with the dog and fries on the counter. He pushes a service bell, pushes the bell again, and then removes an uncooked dog from a lower compartment. When the woman remains seated, I realize the food belongs to the man on the payphone nearby.

A liquor bottle shakes on top of the payphone as he leans against it. He yells in Spanish into the phone. His outfit clashes with the Detroit heat: black skullcap, camouflage army jacket, and camouflage pants. The materials look thick. The slower I walk, the less Spanish I recognize. The man is not speaking Latin American Spanish or Caribbean Spanish. When we learn to speak, we are translating. I try translating what he's saying, but hunger drags me further away.

While watching the redness in his neck, I snatch his food then smash my body into a pillar, six buildings down from the stand. I peel off the soggy bacon before devouring the dog. Juice drips from the bacon to the sidewalk. I drop it and peek from behind my hiding place. The way the concrete juts out, I can only see from the counter to the sidewalk. The terrifying man isn't lurking there or on the opposite side of the street, but I'm not worried about him. I'm more worried about the woman. I watch her as I shove fries in my mouth. Faintly, I hear the bell ring and the hot dog seller sets another tray on the counter.

Klunk, I hear close by and drop the fries. I see the man searching for the thief down the street. He hits a trashcan with a pipe and disappears, but I hear the destruction of metal on metal.

As I run in the opposite direction, the banging stops. Black letters C, A, M, and E on a marquee slow my steps. R and A follow, and then store, and my feet stop altogether. His face does not appear when I look for him. Through the thick graffiti on the window, the world inside looks antique, like a snow globe turned over, and fifty years of stillness has fallen. The front door, covered with wood planks, is nailed tight. I run into the side alley to check for another entrance. At first unrecognizable, I realize the back door has been painted the same dark red as the entire side of the building and then graffitied over. Feeling the door, I figure out it has a wood frame, and it swings toward the inside of the store. I kick the door three times, focusing on the tiny space below the doorknob. Whack, the frame splinters. I kick it again, and the store welcomes me inside.

Peeling paint and plaster and pieces of the cottage cheese ceiling cover the floor. On other sections, it appears as if loaves of moldy bread were ground to crumbs then tossed down for dead pigeons. The crumbs are the color as maggots. At my feet, I see pigeon droppings, white bird feathers, beetle carcasses, and decades of decay. A pillbug crawls out of a square-shaped object. The storefront has built-in shelves on each wall and four display cases. Two cases, closer to the window, are like a broken V with a ten-foot gap in-between them. In the center, sits a waist-high circular case. A longer case is in the back, where the cash register would've been. On the top, propped up, there is a face that haunts me. It is Richard Avedon's photograph of Marian Anderson. Even caked in dust I hear her singing. Dried oak leaves, a wooden box, a golf ball-shaped mineral, a brass candleholder, and a glass bowl are beside her. The arrangement of the items suggests it is an altar. A puckered sign, written in black marker, and taped to the back wall reads, "Do Not Enter Area." The sign reminds me of religious spaces, where only religious leaders are allowed to enter. The sign is a warning. Through time and abandonment, the entire store has become sacred. Air, water, dust, and cobwebs have magnified its preciousness. I trace the shape of a cross on my body. In my left pocket, I fish around finding: keys, tape, lens cap, shower cap, change, knife, and film canister. I grab the canister, kiss it, and add it to the altar. It has a thin strip of correction fluid. The cracked white material has the same innocent appearance as the datura flower. My ancestors in Cuba used it for centuries to induce visionary dreams to reveal the roots of misfortune. The first museum in the town, where my mother's family is from, was a church. Churches can be museums, and museums can be churches. The sign, "Do Not Enter Area" could read, "Do Not Touch The Exhibit." This space could be both a museum of death and a cathedral of life everlasting. I feel safe here.

I try to imagine how the shelves would have looked alive with Nikons, Canons, Minoltas, Leicas, Yashicas, and Fujis. What the skin of the camera bodies would feel like to my fingers? I would wait in wonder for the morning light to open and know one would sell. The saddest image for a photographer to see has to be an abandoned camera store.

My foot brushes against something spongy. Pictures printed on postcards overflow out of the box beside the case. I tap the bottom. A clump of slimy mush and a second Marian slip into dust. As I flip through the familiar McCurrys, Langes, Evans, Erwitts, Adams, and Halsmans, my camera bag tilts. My business cards spill. I caught the bus to pass them out at the DIA – in hopes of making money.

Behind me, the door creaks open. The wind, I assume. More light tiptoes inside. A black flash on the side of my face turns into camouflage pants. Tall and lanky, scraggly dark hairs from the terrifying man's mustache curl down to his upper lip. His crooked nose has a pronounced bump in the middle. A shadow across his eyes forces his face into a permanent scowl.

"You stole from me," he yells in a thick accent. Then he smashes his pipe against the display case. "Now I'm going to steal from you. Give me your camera."

I yell, "no," matching his rage and run behind the case.

"Give it to me. Or I'll kill you," he yells. The man slams the pipe against the glass and glass shatters.

Shoving the camera into my bag, I zip it closed and step backward. I feel the wall. He runs toward me, but the face I see is of my father.

Chapter 31

Through the dust cloud, Father rushes toward me with a machete to hack up my body. Fire will burn the guts, gristle, and fat. My bones and ashes can add to the altar. He kicks a dry rotted chair into the cracked case I'm using as a shield. The sound of glass crunching transforms Father back into the terrifying man. I run to the left. The man screams. I hear a faint shriek, possibly from a rat crushed under his weight. He slips backward. The whole room shakes. White cottage cheese flakes, from the ceiling, fall and float in the air. Pieces catch sunlight and shimmer. I run for the door. As I reach the end of the case, something solid whacks the back of my head. I fall face down in a puddle of pigeon droppings and a clammy green substance. Whatever the green is, it tastes salty on my lips. A rustling noise forces me up to my feet. An O-shaped object hits brick. It smashes and becomes dry oatmeal. His shadow enlarges on the wall. Over my shoulder, an object swings close to my head. The swoosh stings my ear. I squat low, missing the pipe and run behind the case into the corner. A chunk of glass shatters to the ground.

A murky glass bottle rolls against my shoe. The man spotted with dust holds the pipe beside his face as he runs closer to me. I hurl the bottle at him and hit his hand. The glass explodes on contact and the pipe drops. Dust flies up in the damp air. Four rats scatter and disappear. I run for the door. The strap of my camera bag catches on something sticking out of the wall. The rough-textured strap snaps. My shoulder burns from a cut. It felt like a sharp nail. Something close-by crackles. A glob of goo, packed like a snowball, explodes in my face, and I trip. Coughing violently, I wipe my face with the inside of my shirt. The goo smells like spoiled fish left by the owners when they abandoned the store.

He snatches me up to my feet, the way Father snatched me out of bed and dragged me into the bathroom. His hands clench around my throat. Up close, his face is even more terrifying. He bares his teeth. His jaw, square and sharp-angled, seems capable of opening and devouring a man whole. He bites down on my neck. I raise my knee to knee him in between his legs. He bites deeper. Blood dribbles down my neck. I dig into my pant pocket. The knife handle feels like freedom. I stab him in the stomach. He winces, and watching him contort charges my body with pure energy.

"You bitch," he says, but it's Father's face I see on his shoulders.

His eyes follow the blade, up in the air, down to his shoulder. I stab him, and I want to experience the sensation again; how his shoulder opens, and blood oozes out. I stab him again. Blood rushes between my legs. The rush feels like I'm speeding downhill on a sled. His skin peeks out as patches of dust vanish, eaten by perspiration. Under the dust, his face turns pale as death. He presses his wounded shoulder. Blood bleeds between fingers, over grayness and camouflage. My breathing stops from the shock. I run out to the alley, out to the street, into the sun.

The image of the jacket splattered with blood swirls in my head. Green and black and brown and red. The camouflage crumbles when flashing lights drown the street. A police officer must've seen how I looked, running, holding a knife. I slip the knife in my pocket, but it's too late. I see myself as the officer sees me with blood sprayed over my shirt. We make eye contact, but the siren wails are for someone else. In the silence, I rub my hands together to wipe off the blood. Only soap and water will burn off the memory of the knife in his shoulder. Is this what Reed wanted me to discover? How of the languages we speak, violence is the most comfortable. I am Reed's son. Reed is Grandfather's son. In vacation pictures, keloids cover Grandfather's neck, chest, and arms. When I was younger, he loved to tell me how my great grandfather beat him so much that welts formed everywhere on his body, even between his legs. And, that made him fearless.

Another police car, distant but fast approaching, whines and its lights bounce off the buildings. I take off running down the cross street cradling my camera in one arm. My foot kicks a pop can. A man covered in tattoos throws up a gang sign from the side of a building. The three-finger pyramid covers Chicago's Southside. A five-pointed star crown gleams above his bald head. To his left, a crescent moon is made of the word terror. Two thick fonts squeeze thinner fonts in the middle. The word, aardvark, drawn out in a dripping font, cuts off his shoulders. The spray paint is red. The highlighting is in maroon and gold. The word has a snout and with its snout, it sucks up tiny words. A knife stabs him in the shoulder. Cooing pigeons fly past the pyramid. The knife drops to the sidewalk, softens, and turns into bird droppings.

Out of breath, I collapse at a storefront. My hands squeak on the glass as they slip. Five mannequins stick out their tongues in the display. I blink and lean closer to the window. Not to see the blood, the filth, the bite mark, to see the second thumb. It has grown on my right hand, the same hand as Reed. I lift up my hand. No, it's an illusion. Confused, I lower it, and the thumb returns. The display is creating the illusion. Although, from this angle, it's clear I am becoming a shadowy reflection of Reed. I am capable of anything too – even death. As I marry the images in my head, the terrifying man appears. I reach for his face; however, I touch the glass. Did I kill him?

Chapter 32

The bones in Reed's knees crack and pop, the opening ceremony of his ritual. Readjusting himself on the couch, he places a box of fried chicken, two sides, and a greasy paper bag on the tray table. Spicy and salty smells waft through the window crack. He gorges down the meat, potato salad, and biscuits in seven minutes. As he opens the second container, the top flips over and slides down his leg. *Slop*, I hear, and he shoves red beans into his mouth. Sauce spills on his robe. The idea of eating forms a knot in my gut. Standing in the bushes, I read Reed's receipt to avoid being disgusted more. Next, he'll eat the marshmallows, candy bar, donuts, pie, ice cream, and cookies. The paper dropped to the mat when he pulled out his keys. I shiver from the night breeze that rustles the leaves. An odor in the air has me grasping for words. The purple-leaved bush smells livery and rusty.

The living room light and the night sky hide me. As I watch Reed, he watches television. An unseen hand slices open a mutilated stomach on the screen. The abstract image comes into sharper focus. It is of lips painted pale pink and flaunted against a swirling pink background. He blows into a tissue. Redness spreads over white. A sour taste forms in my mouth. My mouth waters. I turn to the television; fixate on the swirling pink blob and everything in my stomach comes up.

Having devoured the rest of the food, half an hour later, Reed is snoring with a football game muted. I sneak out of the bushes, to the side, and push up the dining room window. Inch by inch, I open it and stop every few seconds listening for movement. I ease my right leg inside. Then, I lower my left leg in the window. *Squeak*, the sound surprises me, and I almost slip on a toy. The couch creaks. Waiting six minutes, I then creep over to Reed. His black robe combined with the white, from his shirt, gives him a priest-like appearance. Two bloody tissues are beside his feet. The sauce splattered across his stomach resembles blood. His loud snoring walks up behind me on the stairs.

A concert of two-beat tapping from an insect passes through Junior's bedroom. He's asleep on his side. Even in the dark, a scar on his arm from a fight with Reed is visible.

"Wake up."

"Carsten. What's wrong?"

"I stabbed a man. I thought he was going to kill me."

"Where did you stab him?"

"His stomach."

"God damn! Did you kill him?"

"I don't know. I just ran."

"Did he run after you?"

"I don't remember."

"If I stabbed a man, I'd remember him chasing after my ass. We need a plan. How about we take my car, drive to Wisconsin and disappear."

"That's not a plan."

"You might have killed a man."

"Can you drive me to the studio? I need to sleep then I can decide what to do."

"Stay here tonight and I promise Reed won't know you're here."

Tears come. Junior hugs me. I struggle under the weight of his softness. Words collapse around us, and a stairway materializes. Like a smudge of charcoal on newsprint, with additional strokes a life drawing forms. We have created a connection, closeness, which is more important to brothers than blood or history. Junior knuckle-punches me in the arm, and I punch him back. Then, we growl like bears with our heads raised, a flash from our childhood. A guttural bark, from the back of his throat, makes me laugh. He reverses into bed, yanking the sheets over his head, and says, "good night little brother bear." I creep into the comfort of the room where I used to sleep. My body sinks into the lumpy mattress. Junior had owned this bed before it became mine. The stale sweat odor on my pillow smells welcoming. Even the rough lint balls against my legs feel pleasant. Sleeping on cheap sheets is a luxury compared to lying awake in pain in a sleeping bag. While staring out the window, a cloud shaped like a stomach forces me to flip over, but the ice crystals become real like the bloody tissues downstairs and the image dangles in my head. Sleep comes, eventually.

A bird flapping its wings against a window wakes me in the morning. The bird chirps. Then, a flock of birds follows the first. As I lie in bed, I notice someone has unhung a photograph I shot and propped it against the wall. In the picture, the best man at a Somali wedding hands the groom a silk cummerbund. The red material swallows the bottom half of the groom's stomach. I have to look away. The doorknob clicks. As I watch it turn, I slide the knife from under my pillow. The door opens halfway as my feet touch the carpet. My brother squeezes through the crack. I slide the knife back under the pillow.

"Shhhh," Junior whispers, tiptoeing to the bed. He hands me a sheet of paper, growls to disrupt the silence, and sneaks back out.

The scribbled note reads: *Reed is leaving in twenty minutes for a wedding in Detroit. Be quiet as possible. Both Ricky and I are going.*

Exactly twenty minutes later, I hear *tucka tucka tucka tucka* as Reed reverses out of the driveway. I laugh looking out the window, knowing Junior is in tears listening to the new sound. As the car disappears, Brett appears on the side of his house. Bits of cement cover his arms, jeans, T-shirt, and a pink bandana around his forehead. His curly hair is slicked back into a ponytail with the end puffed out. He waves neither overjoyed nor unexcited and points toward the front door. I kick my bloodied shirt from yesterday under the bed, change into a clean shirt, and then jog downstairs.

Pat, pat, pat, bits fall to the ground in the embrace. His neck smells like wet pebbles. Cement stuck to his shirt scratches my face. His fingers smooth out knots in my back. As we let go, I notice long hairs sticking out around his Adam's apple.

"Where have you been?"

"Reed kicked me out."

"I'm sorry that happened to you. At least he allowed you to come back."

"He didn't. He doesn't know I'm here. I'm leaving in a few minutes."

"Where are you staying now?"

"At the studio."

"Your getting kicked out is my fault. What can I do to help you?"

"It's not and nothing. But something happened yesterday."

Brett's face twitches into a tortured grimace after I finish telling him everything. "You need to turn yourself in."

"I can't. You know what will happen to me."

"It was self-defense. Nothing's going to happen to you."

"I stole from a man and stabbed him. I'm not innocent."

"What if he's dead?"

"And what if he isn't?"

"It has to be tearing you up not knowing what happened. Let's drive there. See if he walked out."

"Then what?"

"You decide what happens next."

"Okay, I can do that," I say to him. However, I know turning myself in would be like holding out my hand to a scorpion and not expecting a sting. All Africans know that the sting of a scorpion burns deeper than the lash of a whip. Under every stone, a scorpion sleeps and under every police station roof, Black men bleed.

Chapter 33

Dark, almost purple, blood splatters color in a shoe print by the entrance. The print, with wavy lines, is identical to the new prints that my shoes have left. More blood, but a smaller amount, is clumped where I stood and knifed the man. Brett points a canister of pepper spray out in front of him as he creeps around the display case with the altar. A church bell rings five times outside. What an odd location for a church. Every other building on this block looks dilapidated. Rolling wheels on the sidewalk crack the silence that follows the bells. High heels click on the pavement. The woman's infant cries. My foot touches the remains of a mop head. The yarn, now blackened, resembles a child's hair. Staring at the mop head, I invent a life for the terrifying man. What if the man collapsed on the street and died and left behind a child?

"I want to turn myself in."

"Okay, let's go."

The fear I felt yesterday somehow masked the smell of urine and sewage in the alley. I lift up the inside of my shirt at the collar to cover my nose and mouth. As I look left, before crossing the street, I see an angel. The statue is abstract, life-size, and four-sided. It resembles a torch, with a slender lower half and bulbous wings. The wings, painted with feathers, surround the statue. The feathers touch the words Baptist Church on a repurposed office building. A few feet away from the angel, I recognize a parked car with dent marks.

While pointing, I tell Brett, "That's Reed's car. I should tell him what happened first. Then we can go."

Behind us, a man yells, "Hey."

Brett and I ignore the yelling and continue walking. A gunshot throws me off balance. I duck down low and flat-backed, sprinting to a car covered in graffiti.

"Come out or I'll shoot your friend."

My stomach drops to my feet. The man that I knifed shoves a gun in my face. His pale face looks monstrous. Thick white spittle drips down the creases of his mouth. His nostrils flare out. About eight pink rings are under his eyes. His bleached hair is disheveled, sticky-looking, with random black strands.

"Walk to the store," the terrifying man says. "Both of you."

"No," a different man screams from further down the street.

The terrifying man yells a Spanish curse word at the other man.

When the other man screams again, I recognize his voice. Reed throws his body in front of me and says, "Take my wallet and leave us alone."

The second gunshot is similar in sound to a heavy-duty dumpster lid slammed shut. Reed collapses to the ground on his back in his church shirt and pants. I slide my hand under his head and catch the blood. His left earlobe is missing as if someone held a hot comb over his blackened ear, and the earlobe burnt off. Above the missing lobe, the burned skin is blistered and swollen. Blood covers his neck and shoulder.

"Help," I yell.

"Shut up," the man screams and kicks my arm.

He bashes Brett across his head with his gun. Brett falls forward, but catches himself. He cross-punches Brett in the gut with his free hand. His hands are also weapons. Brett's knees drop to the ground. The man hops up on his left leg, swinging his right leg high behind him. The kick cracks Brett's side.

"Up," he yells at Brett and he digs the gun barrel into the back of my head. "Get him." He motions the gun between Father and me.

I place Father's arm around my shoulder. Brett repeats this, standing on the opposite side. A fine mist of blood covers my right arm. Maroon blotches break out on both my arms. Father's breathing becomes heavier as we lift him up to his feet. We move, as hand puppets, obedient and without objection, into the camera store. Then, we ease Father onto the floor and prop him against the wall parallel to the entrance.

"Sit," the man says.

Brett sits to my left, positioning me in the middle of him and Father. The terrifying man motions with the gun for me to stand.

Father starts to say something, coughs instead and spits blood on the floor. "Let my son and that boy go."

Brett grips my hand. A movement from the corner of my eye becomes the gun. The gun flies back in the air and forward. Father's head bangs against the wall. Fear and dust burn my eyes. Father doesn't move, and I can't hear him breathing. The man cracks him in the head again with the gun.

"Stop," I yell.

"Up," the man screams.

The church bell rings five times, and the man turns away.

Brett sets a compact object in my hand. "Back pocket. Don't look," he whispers and rolls my fingers over it.

I tuck the object in my pocket without the man seeing. Something crunches under my shoe. My knees start to wobble as I walk, and then my entire body shakes. The man snatches the back of my neck. Our noses almost touch. His eyes are unhuman, wild, like a feral dog that is suspicious of an unfamiliar man.

"No," comes out from somewhere inside of my mouth.

His hand, high in the air, swoops down at my face like a predatory bird, hungry for a kill. The gun cracks me in the jaw. I stumble back, dizzy, falling, but not falling, the violent pain swelling in my head. The man yanks my arm toward him.

"Stop," Father yells.

A bullet lodges into the wall an inch above his head. With the man's back facing me, I see a second gun tucked in the back of his pants. I wrap my fingers around the object in my pocket. His head turns to the side as if sensing my movement. I jump, almost flying like a daredevil cliff diver, throwing out my arms. I wake up with his throat clamped in the bend of my arm. He yells an unfamiliar word in

Spanish. I pull him back toward my body and push down the pepper spray nozzle. The gun flies back. I tighten my elbow-grip around his throat. His finger pulls back on the trigger. Fire, real fire, like a campfire, glowing orange, shoots out of the barrel. My ears ring. He thrashes around as I continue spraying him in the face. The gun drops to the floor, and he wails. White flakes from the ceiling flutter over us and dust rises from the floor. Brett hurries and grabs the gun. I cough, having inhaled pepper spray. The man claws at his face. Brett jabs him in the gut and punches him again and again.

The man stomps down on my shoe with his back heel crushing my toes. I squeeze my elbow tighter around the man's neck, hoping he loses consciousness. His head slumps forward. Blond hair slams in my face. I hear a cracking noise. Every color in the room is sucked out, and every object, even the people, turns white. The whites bleed into each other and become one image. Teeth bite into my arm. I punch where his head should be and hit bone. I hear a fist punch and shoving. A piece of glass falls and shatters. Rising dust irritates my nose, and I sneeze. A scraping sound outside of the door startles me. Someone else is coming into the store. I step backward and slip on something round.

Like a white light switched on in the darkroom, the colors return. The man knees Brett in between his legs. Brett squeals, holds himself, collapses to his knees, and falls over into a pile of cottage cheese flakes. Father, his face wrinkled cabbage, clutches his neck in desperation. The man's eyes are slits. More spit drips from his mouth. He pulls his leg back to kick Brett on the ground. I push him to stop the kick. The man punches me in the chest and grabs the other gun tucked in the back of his pants. He raises the gun. Glass explodes. More light comes into the store. Then, another gun is shot. Blood gushes down the man's shoulder.

"Drop it," an unseen man with a husky voice yells through the open door.

The husky-voiced man steps into the store with his gun pointed at the man. Two more police officers, also in bulletproof vests, rush in after him. The man turns his head toward the sound of the officer's voice.

Seeing a pipe on the ground, I grab it and smash the pipe across his back.

"Police, freeze," the officer yells. "Drop your weapon."

Slowly, I pull Brett by his shirt to the wall. Father struggles to stand and leads us, hunch-backed, behind the closest glass case. A long string of watery snot dribbles from the man's nose.

"Don't think. Do it," the female officer shouts.

The man screams, lowers the gun, and the officer rushes him. The man coughs violently; the coughing turns into wailing. His skin turns gray. He gags. Another male officer, not in gear, takes the man, in handcuffs and pushes him out the door.

Squeak, rattle, squeak, announces two paramedics before they run in wheeling a stretcher.

"You're going to be okay," the husky-voiced officer says to Father.

I sit cross-legged beside Father on the floor. His blood glues my underwear to my thighs. He grabs my hand and blood and dirt squishes between our fingers. Blood soaks the top half of his shirt. Two cuts are on his forehead. His fingernails look bluish from the dust. Through photography, I learned faith is the meaning of love between men. If faith deepens through prayer, photography is our prayer. I start praying. Who would I be without photography: someone else's child? Without photography, I wouldn't have worked for the Chicago Tribune or the Chicago Defender newspaper. Without my cameras, I would not have bothered telling Father I loved him every night when I lived with him because that would've been a lie. I love him because he has given me purpose and an occupation. I have seen the world through countless cameras, and I'm made of all that I have seen. I am a photographer. Eye to camera to print.

The paramedic slides two gloved fingers down his neck. He twitches and bites his lip. His bottom lip bleeds. He squeezes my hand harder. His glassy eyes focus on something by his feet.

"Pick that up," he says weakly and breathes through his mouth using his whole rib cage. His lips seem pasty gray; however, it does not appear that dust is on his lips.

Under pellets that look like salt crystals, the white of my business card shines. Light flickers as I hand him the card. Light coming in from outside reflects on the display case. In the broken glass, the scene is multiplied. Father's body shivers and I realize his brown skin is pale under the dust. A rattling sound comes out from the back of his throat.

"I love you," Father says and stares at me with enlarged pupils as if staring through my body.

Hearing those words, "I love you," the shock is so incredible that I squash his hand in a death grip, and I continue squeezing even when his hand loses its warmth.

Acknowledgements

Many thanks to the Otis College Graduate Writing Program, Beyond Baroque Fiction Workshop, the City of West Hollywood, West Hollywood Library, the Ann Arbor District Library, and Tishuan Scott for your generous support.

Specifically, I would like to thank my writing workshop instructors Peter Gadol, Sarah Shun-lien Bynum, Jen Hofer, and Honoree Jeffers for pushing me past the ordinary to delight in the unexpected, to reach for strange-sounding words, and to write with an unusual magic. To my unofficial instructors, Staceyann Chin, Michelle Tea, Daphne Gottlieb, Samuel R. Delany, Mattilda Bernstein Sycamore, Yusef Komunyakaa, and Toni Morrison, thank you for your guidebooks to writing.

Diana Robertson, Paul Vangelisti, Daniel Lazar, David Groff, Hank Hendersen, Michael Che, Keith Boykin, Jeffrey King/In The Meantime, Winnie McCroy, Jason St. Amand, Raspin Stuwart, Kara Mondino, Joel Garcia, Laura Manchester, Kurt Thum, DJ Baker, L.R., and Antonio G.

©GAREN HAGOBIAN

Victor Yates was raised in Jacksonville, Florida and now lives in Los Angeles. His work has appeared in Windy City Times, Gorgeous, and Edge. As a graduate of the Creative Writing program at Otis College, he is the recipient of an Ahmanson Foundation grant. He is the winner of the Elma Stuckey Writing Award (1st place in poetry). Two of his poems were included in the anthology, "For Colored Boys," which was edited by Keith Boykin. The anthology won the American Library Association's Stonewall Book Award. Also, he has taught writing workshops at the University of Southern California (for the Models of Pride Conference), Job Corps, Whaley Middle School (Compton), Gindling Hilltop Camp (Malibu), and Bright Star Secondary Charter Academy (Inglewood). This is his first novel.

CPSIA information can be obtained at www.ICGtesting.com
Printed in the USA
LVOW08s2254100716

495776LV00006B/411/P